Emil

Get # CRUSHED !

A Hockey Love Story

XO

VEGAS CRUSH #1

BRIT DeMILLE

Brit DeMiller

Copyright © 2018 Brit DeMille
All rights reserved.
ISBN: 1719159122
ISBN-13: 978-1719159128
Cover Design: *Designs by Dana*
Cover Image: *Sara Eirew*

AUTHORS NOTE

This story is the debut novel from Brit DeMille. Writing a sports romance was something I'd wanted to do for a very long time, in collaboration with my husband—sports fanatic extraordinaire. So, seven months ago, on a complete whim, we decided to write a hockey romance instead of a baseball one, and also to set our fictional team in Las Vegas. Since it was brand new territory for the hockey world in general, with the newest expansion team—the *Vegas Golden Knights*—starting up for their very first season in the NHL, we figured there wouldn't be a lot of back history to compete with for our fictional **VEGAS CRUSH** team, and it would be a fun world to place our characters in by having them working and living in fabulous Sin City.

Crafting the story for CRUSHED was done while watching many a hockey game, but especially while following along as the *Vegas Golden Knights* won games. And kept winning. And kept on winning; fighting their way to the top of the standings in game...after game...after game.

Flash forward to late May 2018. The *Vegas Golden Knights* have won the Western Division and are in the freaking finals for the Stanley Cup! Watching their rise has been crazy fun. An unexpectedly thrilling adventure for fans of a real Las Vegas hockey club which has grabbed the attention of the entire world with their fairytale of triumph in a brand new arena. It's the stuff that romance novels are made of. Quite literally.

Writing in the fictional universe of the **VEGAS CRUSH** has been the highlight of my year, and I hope you enjoy this small peek into Evan and Holly's wonderful world as much as we did writing it.

Happy reading!

♥ Brit & Mr. D

BRIT DeMILLE

DEDICATION

For those who are,
and always will be...
VEGAS STRONG.

ONE

Holly

J ust one step outside and I have to turn myself right back around again.

As I return inside to grab some darker shades and a water, I remind myself yet again that I now live in the Mojave Desert. An extra water could mean the difference between life and death at some point in my future. Best to always be prepared.

It's crazy to think about going into an ice hockey rink when it's easily pushing 100 degrees on this late September day. Of course, I haven't really been in an ice hockey rink, apart from the two times I interviewed with the Las Vegas Crush. I guess I'd better get used to the odd juxtaposition between the Las Vegas desert climate and the seemingly endless winter of the hockey world.

My condo is situated in a totally vanilla suburb that's about a fifteen-minute drive to the very non-vanilla Strip. The hockey arena sits on the edge of all of the insanity. I've learned that most Las Vegas natives barely ever see the Strip, unless they work there. Apart from all the lights and fountains and casinos, Las Vegas is a pretty normal place.

I guess I shouldn't be surprised at that. Having grown up in Los Angeles, I know all about how to ignore the tourist traps.

As I make the quick commute—one of the best parts about this move, since LA traffic is just as bad as people say it is—I blast some music, dancing and singing my way into my assigned parking spot. Still humming, I gather my bag and pull on my suit jacket before heading into the arena to observe my first practice.

My uncle Troy is a scout for the Crush. He played hockey professionally until he was well into his thirties, then started scouting once a knee injury put him out of commission for play. He called me two months before I graduated UCLA's Communication Studies program, asking me if I'd be interested in interviewing for a social media position with the Crush. He thought it might be a good fit, since I'm an athlete. At first, I balked—I'm a distance runner and I've never been to a single hockey game—but once I learned about the job, it sounded great. I interviewed, and much to my surprise, was hired. So here I am, a hockey neophyte, LA expatriate, heading to my first day of work with the Vegas Crush.

And there he is. Tall and broad-shouldered, my uncle is still a handsome guy. He shares my dad's side of the family's ginger hair, a little grey on the sides, and blue eyes. I, of course, got the brown hair and brown eyes of my mom's side of the family.

He pulls me into a hug, patting me on the back with enough vigor that I pull away laughing. "Hey," I say, "I'm not choking. No need for violence."

"Sorry, sorry," he says, grinning. "I'm just so excited that you're here. And damn proud of you. Do you know how many people want to get their foot in the door in sports marketing? And you beat out people who know way more about hockey than you do. You must be pretty damn good with this social media business."

"Well, I'm pretty sure that *Social Media Manager* is, like, the lowest on the totem pole, and I'm sure being related to their star scout probably didn't hurt, but it's a great start and I'm really excited to get going. I have lots of ideas for how we can engage fans and connect them to the players via the different platforms," I say. "Thanks for thinking of me. Now you're totally on the hook for making sure I know enough by opening day to not bomb."

2

"Interns are actually lowest on the totem pole, not anyone with the title of manager," he corrects, elbowing me. He points me in the direction of the arena and starts walking. "And I am more than happy to begin your hockey education. I know enough for the both of us."

"Well, you should be out scouting so I can't rely on all that knowledge if it's locked up in your big brain. Spill it, uncle." I love to joke around with him.

"Oh, Holly-dolly," he says, using the name he's called me since I was a little kid, "always so bossy."

"Well," I do have *manager* in my title, as you pointed out."

Troy laughs at this. "So, the arena can also be called the *barn*. There are lots of slang terms that you'll hear the guys say. Some are appropriate, and some are not, so talk to me if you're not sure what something means before you use it publicly."

"Wait, hockey players can say inappropriate things? I'm shocked, Uncle Troy."

He chuckles and shakes his head. As we walk in, players are already on the ice.

"Shouldn't I head to HR?" I ask.

"They'll be ready for you whenever we're finished down here. It's a Sunday, so it'll be a paperwork day. They'll show you your cubicle, get you set up on a computer and whatnot, but not much else until tomorrow."

"Ah," I say. "Okay."

We take seats in the third row from the glass. "It's the end of rookie training week," he explains. "It's actually a really good day to be here, because now the other team members will come out and scrimmage the rookies. Should be fun to watch."

We watch as the more seasoned players take the ice. As the action starts, I find myself fascinated by the quick pace of the game. But I understand very little about what's going on. Troy explains as things occur, pointing out when someone smothers the puck, or when a call is made for icing. He talks about the power play as a rookie gets put into the penalty box.

It's a lot, honestly, and I take notes, but decide I'm going to have to get some books, and maybe just watch like a thousand hockey games on YouTube before tomorrow morning.

At one point, two huge guys crash against the glass. I jump as it rattles, but Troy lets out a "Whoop!" that tells me this is quite normal and probably fun for the audience. The larger of the guys, from the veteran team, pushes the rookie. There's a little tussle that causes both of their helmets to fall onto the ice.

The two players, red-faced and wet-haired, battle it out until finally, the coach blows his whistle and skates over. There's a verbal argument. The rookie says the older player checked him on purpose. The non-rookie tells him to grow a pair and asks if he's ever played hockey before.

I watch, rapt attention on the battle between two guys who are supposed to be teammates. The coach says what I'm thinking, "You two better kiss and make up. You're on the same team, for fuck's sake."

The rookie shrugs and reaches down for his helmet, skating away. But the bigger one? He looks at Troy and me. Well, he looks at me, because our eyes meet, and I swear I feel it all the way down into places unmentionable. He's frowning, which isn't the expression I want to see when a hot guy checks me out, but still, there's a weird charge between us. And it lasts all of twenty seconds before he spits on the ice— gross—grabs his helmet, and skates toward the penalty box.

"Phew...that was intense."

"All part of the game," Troy says. "These are good guys, hard workers, but they do get competitive. Even with each other. And the older players always feel like they need to toughen the younger players up. It's a thing."

"Who was the guy who stared a hole through us?"

"Evan Kazmeirowicz," he says. "He came to us a year ago, played so well they gave him a multi-year, multi-million-dollar contract."

"So, he's barely out of rookie-hood, himself," I comment.

"From an NHL sense, I guess, but not really." Troy says. "He's been bred to play hockey. Grew up in Ukraine. Played on the Ukraine Olympic hockey team for the first time when he was, like, eighteen. Played again at twenty-two, then came to the States to play minor league hockey. Got recruited here last year and just tore some shit up."

"Did you scout him?"

"I did," he says like a proud dad. "He was the team's leading scorer last season. Plays left wing, or forward is another name for it. He's born to score."

Yes, he is. But I keep my mouth shut because I know it will only make it more obvious that my lady parts are on fire after that weird stare-down.

"C'mon," Troy says. "Let's get you upstairs so you'll be all set for tomorrow,"

I stand and follow my uncle out of the arena. Just because I'm a glutton for punishment, I turn back and glance at the penalty box, only to find Evan Kazmeirowicz staring right back.

Yep. I am in trouble.

TWO

EVAN

My concentration has officially been fucking broken. I was in the zone, ready to pummel some rookies into submission when I look over and see the prettiest pair of pouty lips I ever wanted to meet. Or kiss. Or do a whole list of things with.

With dark hair in a long ponytail, dark eyes, and those luscious pouty lips I'd like to plunder for days, she's got my full attention. I sincerely hope she's a recruiter because no player who likes pussy would ever say no to playing for a team where that beauty works.

She looks back at me as she leaves and I legit want to jump the barrier, skate to the glass, and beg her to let me sink my biscuit into her net. Somehow, though, I think this might get me fired. Or kicked in the balls. No one needs that.

As soon as my penalty time ends, I get my head back in the game, playing hard until Coach splits us up for drills. Of course, because Coach Roger Brown doesn't like drama and bullshit, he pairs me with the young rookie.

The drill we run requires us to do short passes back and forth while we make our way from one end of the ice to the other. The tight set of the kid's lips and jaw tell me he's still pissed about the way I checked him earlier.

"Kid, let it go. Part of the game."

"Whatever, yeah," he grunts, his English good despite a thick, Russian accent.

"What's your name?"

"Mikhail," he says after a moment as if he's deciding whether or not to grace me with a response. *Punk.*

"Is that your first or last name?"

"First."

"How old are you?"

"Eighteen."

I gather one-word answers are all I'll be getting because not only is he a punk-ass teen, but also a rookie, and he doesn't want to be told a damn thing. I guess it'll be up to Coach to work that chip off his shoulder, but I get it. He's probably banking on a good year or two, followed by a multi-year contract that will set up his family for years. It's a common story for these kids who come straight to the NHL as teenage phenoms. There's a great deal of pressure to perform well.

We move to other drills which include passing for distance and shooting on the fly. Coach yells, "Shots on goal! Shots on goal!" This is his mantra. He wants us to take shots, and then take more shots. If we don't take shots on goal, we won't score.

After practice, we head in for feedback from the coaching staff. Nothing major just yet, since we're all just getting to know each other. Some of the guys head to the showers, but I hit the gym with my buddy Georg to lift some weights.

He spots me on the bench, of course threatening to let the thing drop on my head.

"I should fire you," I say, grunting at the weight. I've been pushing myself hard in the weight room lately. I want to be in top physical shape this season. No contract slump for me."

"As your friend, or as your teammate, or as your spotter?" he asks, grinning.

"All of the above," I answer with a sharp exhale of breath on my fifth rep. "You suck. Your suckage is overwhelming me right now."

"Speaking of suckage," Georg says. "You'll probably be able to get any woman you want on her knees now that you're making the big bucks."

"No need for money," I say. "My cock is a beacon with or without a wallet full of cash."

"Indeed," Georg says. "You'll have to get bodyguards to fend off all those bunnies. Pussy magnet is what you are."

"Nothing wrong with that," I say, finishing the set. I sit up and take a long swig from my water bottle. "What about you? You still seeing your little waitress? Wasn't her name, Bunny?"

"Bambi," he says. He shrugs. "Every so often. Netflix and chill, you know?"

"How's she feel about that?"

"You're asking about her feelings?" Georg asks, incredulous. "Since when do you give a shit what a woman feels?"

"I care," I say, making a *duh* face. "I'm not heartless."

He rolls his eyes. "You need me anymore? I've got my own workout to do."

I give him the finger as he heads off to the squat rack.

Georg and I have been friends since hitting it off in our first year on the team. He's my road roommate. We're about the same age, which is nice since we're both older than a lot of the guys on the team now. I feel like an old-ass man sometimes, but I feel like this is an all-star year, and I'm gunning for captain next year. I've paid my dues in hockey for longer than some of these boys have been weaned from their mama's titties. Okay, maybe not that long. But long enough. It's time. And Georg is no competition for captain. He drinks too much, and he makes the news too often. Always up to antics with cars, with women, or partying at some sin-den that'll be trending on social within hours. Yeah, Coach's mantra might be *shots on goal*, but *fast cars, fast women* is Georg's at the moment.

Which is not to say I don't like my fair share of the puck bunnies. I do. They are generally very easy to procure, though I prefer not to see anyone more than two or three times. Anything more than that and it looks and acts like a relationship. And I do not want one of those.

Georg does, but he always gets bored about six months in. If I had to guess, Bambi's probably on month seven right about now.

I run three quick miles on the treadmill before pushing myself through the punishing CrossFit workout one of our trainers put up on the board. He switches out the routines every day, with a twelve-minute loop designed, I think, to make us feel like we're dying.

As I wait for Georg to finish up his weight work, I ask, "Did you see the woman who came in with Troy today during scrimmage?"

"Nope. Didn't even notice Troy, the old bastard. Why?"

"She was a hottie," I say smoothly. "I just wondered if they brought her on to scout or something."

"Hot scout?" he asks. "Huh. How's you have time to look her over?"

"When I checked the rookie, I just looked up and there she was."

"Did time slow down for you in that magical moment?" he asks, his voice faux-sweet.

I punch him hard in the arm. "Don't be a dumbass."

"Ow," he says, but he's still grinning. "Well, just find Troy and ask who she is. It's not so hard."

"Yeah, I know. If she's a scout she won't be around much. Might be good for a quickie now and again."

"I guess," Georg says. "I make it a policy not to hump the help, though. Just makes life easier in the long run."

"You're not wrong there, friend. I screwed one of the trainers for the Olympic team once. It was okay, not earth shattering and certainly not good enough for a second round. You would not believe how much pain she inflicted on me in the gym afterward."

We start up a conversation about our times on separate Olympic teams as we head to the showers. Georg grew up playing the same as I did, though he played in the States a lot sooner than I did, and then fumbled around longer in the minor leagues. We got picked up the same year, and he loves to bring up the Olympics. I have no idea why. I mean, it was a good gig and I was super young. Cocksure. A lot like young Mikhail, I suppose. I had a lot of piss and vinegar in me, and something to prove. I took a shit-ton of risks as a player, got injured a lot, played through my injuries.

I'm not exactly conservative now, but I guess I'd say I'm a more thoughtful player now. And having Georg as my right-hand man has been a good match. He's a defender, but he's got his eyes on the goal, too. If he plays as well as he did last season, I'll bet he'll be right there on the all-star team with me.

As I shower and change, most of the guys have left already. I say goodnight to Coach and head out toward the parking lot, finding the sun and heat overwhelming after a day in the barn. I look around, hoping to catch a glimpse of the dark-haired beauty, but no such luck. It's fine, I'll just think about her on my drive home instead.

THREE

Holly

The HR manager was probably miffed to have to come in on a Sunday, so after the paperwork was signed she spent exactly three minutes showing me around before heading out. She leaves me sitting at a laptop in a cubicle with a stack of new employee info to read.

I head home instead because, really, why sit in a dark, empty office on a Sunday if you don't have to. Downside? I'll still know practically zero tomorrow, when I will be expected to work, and there will actually be people around. Upside? It's still early enough in the day that I can enjoy the pool at my complex for a few hours.

When I arrive home, I wonder if I'll ever get tired of walking through my new front door, knowing the place behind that door is mine. It was love-at-first-look for me and my new condo. From the vibrant blue entryway, to the huge kitchen decked out with stainless appliances, to the master bath with a tub big enough for laps, to the grotto shower that can fit at least four people, I was smitten. Not, of course, that I'm adventurous enough to have three other people in the shower with me. I am a one-man-at-a-time kinda girl.

I find an empty lounge chair under an umbrella, laptop in hand, fully intending to watch a bunch of hockey on YouTube. Instead, I find myself Googling "Evan Kazmeirowicz."

Six-foot-three. Damn. I'm tall at five-foot-nine, and he's half a foot taller. I've always had a thing for big dudes and this Evan is a big dude, indeed. I read his stats—led the team in scoring last season, leading to a multi-year contract. Works in tandem with a defensive player named Georg Kolochev. They're both twenty-seven, and both started with the Crush at the same time. Kind of a bosom-buddies thing, as is evidenced by a plethora of photos of the two of them on and off the ice together. The off-ice photos are mostly accompanied by skimpily-dressed young women. Great, two man-whores.

There are a few videos of them talking about their games. Georg's Russian accent is pronounced, where Evan's has more of a British sound to it. It's sexy, no doubt. I'll bet lots of women drop their panties just to hear his voice.

I slam my laptop shut after realizing I've been ogling Evan Kazmeirowicz for more than a half hour. He's on the team. I work for the team. It would not be a good start to my career to have an affair with a player, no matter how hot he is. And no matter how he makes my lady-parts tingle with joy.

Nope. I need to go do my homework and learn about the game of hockey. Bring on the touchdowns!

Kidding.

I MAKE SURE to arrive at the office early the next morning because after lunch, I've arranged to meet Troy for more training on the language and logistics of hockey. Four hours of watching highlights and game clips last night helped some, but the live action instruction from Troy is so much better.

Coffee mug in one hand, I make my way into the office suite, excited to find the place buzzing with activity and feeling completely different than it did on Sunday afternoon. In my cubicle I power up my computer as my boss pops her head in.

"I thought it was you," Fiona Starling says.

She looks sharper than I remember from my interview, in an expensive-looking dress. Her brunette hair is in a blunt bob to her chin and she wears funky eyeglass frames that accentuate the color of her bright blue eyes. Fiona is the media queen behind the Las Vegas Crush. Frankly, she intimidates me, but I'm an athlete and I'm used to intimidating coaches, so I am just viewing her as I would any of my college coaches. Tough, cunning, and hopefully someone I can learn from.

I stand up and shake her hand. "Hi, Fiona, good to see you."

I know I sound too eager but whatever, I'll just go with it.

Fiona smiles but I can tell it's fake. She's probably rethinking her choice to hire me. She says, "So I hear our star scout has been schooling you on the game a bit?"

"Yeah." I clear my throat. "Yes. Troy and I watched a scrimmage yesterday. We're going to meet down at practice this afternoon. I'm eager to start getting some social media traffic going."

"That's what I like to hear," she says. "Well, let me know if you need anything at all."

"Thanks, Fiona."

She walks away without another word.

I spend the morning reading through the social media pages of some of our competitors, getting ideas for how they use platforms to tell stories. I also meet briefly with the folks in the Crush's charitable foundation office to get a sense of which guys are out doing good in the community. Those are awesome stories to use on social media.

When my uncle shows up, I realize I've worked through lunch. Luckily, he's a man of ample resources, so he leads me to one of the arena's many food stands, unlocks a door, and tells me to grab whatever I want. The choices are, of course, junk food or more junk food, so I just grab a water and a candy bar masked as an energy bar before we head back out.

"Are you just allowed to take what you want?" I ask.

"Yeah," he says with a grin. "I bring potential players here sometimes and offer snacks to sweeten the deal."

He makes a face like he's waiting for me to laugh. I frown a little. "Did I miss a joke?"

He elbows me. "Sweeten the deal? Candy?"

I just blink at him.

"Okay, it's Monday. I get it. I'll try harder next time."

We take our seats at center ice. I call it the midline and Troy quickly corrects me to "red line."

"Each period starts with a center ice faceoff," he says. "Faceoff happens after a team scores, as well."

"Oh, like soccer?" I ask.

"Yes, a lot like soccer. In fact, some of our guys are on summer soccer leagues because it's a game with a lot of similar concepts."

"Cool. I dated a soccer player in college."

"Oh yeah?" he asks.

I give a one-shoulder shrug. "Nothing serious, but I did learn a lot watching his games."

I get out my phone and pull up the Twitter account for the team. Fiona gave me full reign on social media posts and asked me to rally the masses to get them excited for pre-season, so I start taking photos with my phone and tweeting them out with Troy's help on captions.

The Team Captain is David Chalamet, a Canadian in his final season with the Crush. Troy tells me he's a fan favorite, and well-known for work he does with the team's charitable foundation.

"I remember they told me about him," I say. "He does a big event each year for kids who have cancer, right?"

"He does," Troy says. "He's a real nice guy, real genuine."

I snap a photo of him on the ice and send it out with a link to his event page on the foundation web-page.

"Are the other guys not as nice?"

"Oh, I think it's like any industry," Troy says. "There's good and bad. They all have ego and talent, but some have more ego than talent. There are a few I wouldn't leave alone with you in an empty room, and at least one I wouldn't leave alone with you in a crowded one."

"Ohhh," I say in a dramatic tone. "A lady killer?"

"They're all lady killers, and one or two who play for the other team, so to speak. Several are married, but it doesn't stop the puck bunnies from giving it the old college try."

"Excuse me...puck bunnies?"

Troy grins. "Sorry, crass term for hockey groupies."

"Indeed. I'm offended on their behalf. Yikes."

"It's one of those terms we don't use on social media, if you didn't already pick that up." I can tell he's trying to keep it light. I can also tell he's a little embarrassed about his use of the term. He clears his throat and says, "Sorry. Been around sports dudes too long."

Troy switches to more hockey specifics, but I tune him out as I thumb out a few more tweets about how the rookies are holding up in scrimmages. I find a few of their stats and toss them out with photos from the stock files.

The team has a Facebook and a Snapchat, as well as an Instagram account. I'm told that we use Snapchat on game days, and I've gotten permission to grab Snapchat images and video while the team heads out to the ice for each game. For now, I just focus on teasing specific team members and their stats.

I snap back to attention when one of my favorite songs plays. It's a Fall Out Boy song called *Immortals*. I start dancing in my chair.

"Like this one?" Troy asks.

"I do. I confess I'm a bit of a pop-punk girl. I always blasted this song when I was running distance."

"It's a good one," he says. "Music is a big part of the hockey experience. And teams are superstitious, so they pick one lead-in song and stick with it pretty much year-after-year. The deejay has a ball, though, matching music to what's going on out there on the ice, and sometimes to what's going on in the stands."

"Like how?" I ask.

"Oh, there's a kiss cam, so when that's going, he might play something goofy and romantic. When there's a really big play, he'll put on something high-energy. The music is meant to help energize the crowd."

I bank this information, figuring I can use the music cues to come up with some fun social media stuff. Like maybe I can match each player with his favorite songs or something. While I'm writing that down in my idea notebook, there's another crash against the glass.

"Paybacks are a bitch!" I hear, and I look up to find the face of Evan Kazmeirowicz smooshed comically against the glass, as the rookie from the day before taunts him mercilessly.

As this scene unfolds, some cheesy, old rock ballad plays. The lyrics are like, "Lady...of the morning...love shines...in your eyes."

Troy is singing along, swaying to the beat and when I side-eye him, he chuckles and says, "Styx, man...never gets old."

I make a face of distaste and shake my head, my attention back to the glass, where Evan and the rookie are tussling again, to the dismay of the coach, who sends them both to the bench to cool down.

Evan skates off, and my stomach gets that lurchy butterfly feeling as I take in his chiseled features, a five o'clock shadow of scruff on his cheeks. His dark hair stands on end as he pulls off his helmet and glares at the other guy.

"Rookie's trying to show he can piss the same distance as the big guys," Troy says. "He'll settle down eventually."

"Does that Evan guy have a temper?" I ask.

"They all do from time to time," Troy says. "Fighting is part of why people pay for seats like these."

"Seems kind of brutal."

"Eh," he grunts with a shrug.

The rest of practice, I alternate between answering tweets, writing down ideas and questions, and checking out hot, hot Evan Kazmeirowicz, who's back on the ice, moving like lightning along the ice during a scoring exercise.

"He's fast," I comment, mostly to myself.

"He's fast indeed," Troy says. "Some wingers are more defensive, but he's an out-and-out scorer. See the guy to his right? He's literally Kazmeirowicz' right hand man. Georg Kolochev is his name. They're a formidable pair."

"Aww, bromance," I say sweetly, making my uncle laugh.

"Write that down in your little book. People will love it."

I giggle but do write it down. I'll have to see what I can find out about their relationship off the ice, but really, I can still do the story with just their on-ice performance.

They do move well together, like a well-oiled machine. At one point, I find myself staring blatantly at the pair, only to realize they're both staring right back at me. The defenseman, Georg, wiggles his eyebrows and elbows his friend, who grins and looks at his skates. I feel my cheeks heat and look quickly down at my phone.

I have got to learn to be around these players without acting like some teenage fangirl. Yikes.

FOUR

EVAN

Preseason game number one is in the books. It wasn't my best game ever, but we won, and I scored twice, so I guess I'll chalk it up as a good start. Of course, I got checked big time because that stupid rookie wasn't in the right spot when I was ready for a pass. If he'd have passed to me when I got to the line, I'd have chucked the biscuit right into the net and scored a third time, but nooo, the motherfucker was showboating, hogging the puck, and it gave too much time for their defensive players to move on me. Bam! Right into the glass, helmet off, taking a beating.

After I shower up and dress, I head out to the postgame press event Fiona has set up. I see the hot brunette across the room with Troy Laurent, the team's best scout. They're together every time I see that chick. So, either he's her silver fox or she's a new scout. I hope against hope it's the latter because…eeeew. I mean, he's all right for an old-timer but damn. What hot, young woman wants old cock when she can have—

"Hi, sexy," a familiar voice says, breaking me out of my thoughts about hot chicks and old balls. It's Kacey King, a local television news personality. Speaking of hot…Kacey is all big tits, blonde hair, and oozing sex in a tight, black dress paired with fuck-me heels.

18

Did I mention I may have boned her? Just once. I mean...look at her. And it was good, maybe more than good, but it was end-of-season and I was a little drunk after our last game...and we just never really connected again after that.

So, it's awkward, sort of, when she puts me on camera right away, her blue eyes sparkling with mischief and invitation as she asks me questions about the preseason and the big hit I took tonight.

"It looked like you were out of sync with the new players a bit," Kacey comments. "Are you concerned about taking another hit in next week's game?"

"Well, we take hits no matter what, but we can definitely stand to play more like a unit. I can take it though, I'm a big boy, and the fans like a good crack at the glass every so often."

"Especially when they get an up-close glimpse of one of Las Vegas's most eligible bachelors," she says with a sexy grin.

"Oh gosh," I say, rubbing my hand over my beard and grinning. "Did that list come out again?"

"No, not yet, but I'm sure your name will be there again this year, though many fans would gladly help you remove yourself from that spotlight."

"Well," I say, looking around the room to look for the mysterious brunette, "You never know when lightning will strike."

She cuts the camera and squeezes my arm. "Hey, good game tonight. Really great to see you."

There's nothing implied about the statement. Nope. It's overt and sexy and if I wasn't trying to make my way through the crowd to mack on someone else, I might give her a time and a place for round two. Operative word being 'might.'

All the local sports journalists are here, so I make nice and dutiful and give them a few sound bites about how we're working on teamwork, learning each other's style of play, adjusting to some new faces, and blah, blah, fucking blah.

I finally get through the crowd to find Coach Brown talking to Troy and that gorgeous brunette. They're having a scouting conversation about some high school phenomenon. Coach is balking.

"Hell no, Troy," he says.

"He's amazing, dude," Troy says. "The next Great One."

"Oh, come on," Coach says with an epic eye roll. "He's a kid. Give him time to season up then bring him to me. I'm not into shiny things."

"Suit yourself," Troy says. "I'll have others for you to look at."

"Yep," Coach says. "Chalamet's gonna leave a hole. Fill it."

I decide this is the time to insert myself into the conversation. "Who needs Chalamet when you've got Kazmeirowicz and Kolochev?" I ask with a wide grin.

"You mean Kazochev?" Troy asks with a snicker.

"Yeah, who came up with that? New social media twerp?" I ask with a laugh.

"You're looking at the...twerp," the brunette says.

My mouth is does its best impression of what-the-fuck and I say nothing. *Fuck me.*

"Evan, this is my niece, Holly Laurent," Troy says with a smirk.

Holly offers her hand to shake. I look at it for a good long while, trying to make sense of what is happening. I need to get my shit together, so I shut my yap, square my shoulders, and shake the young woman's hand.

"I'm—"

"Evan Kazmeirowicz," she interrupts. "I know. I've been promoting you and Kolochev's special on-ice relationship. You have a *ship* name now."

"Kazochev?" I ask. "Was that your idea?"

"The ship name? No." Her cheeks turn a lovely shade of pink as she gives me a rueful smile. "But I definitely capitalized on it once it took shape."

"So, your role at the organization is?"

"Social Media Manager. I'm on Fiona's team."

"Okay," I say. "Well good luck with her. She bites sometimes. You'd better be on your toes. You a big hockey fan?"

"Actually," Troy says, "Holly's a bit of a hockey newbie. She's picking it up pretty fast, though."

"Not a fan of the game?" I ask. "How can you promote the team if you don't have a real appreciation for what we're doing out there?" I hope my tone comes off the way I intend. Teasing. Flirty. A bit of challenge.

Her chin lifts a bit before she responds. "I'm an athlete, too. I'm pretty sure I can keep up."

"From what I've heard, social media traffic is way up already. Seems like you're doing just fine," I say with a wink. "Be good if you knew how to lace up a pair of skates, though."

She lets out a little laugh. Coach takes Troy off to the side to talk scouting some more, so I'm left with Holly. She shifts her mass of long, dark hair over one shoulder and bites her full bottom lip. *I'd like to suck on that lip.*

"I've seen you on the ice. During practice. You and the rookie seem to still be butting heads."

"He's nothing I can't handle. He'll settle down soon enough."

"And you, Evan, when will you settle down?"

I laugh out loud at this. "Well, I might be past the point of no return."

"I think Troy told me you're from the Ukraine, but your accent is more British?"

"Good catch. I went to a British private school in the Ukraine. My mother is American, my father Russian, so I think the result is a bit of a mash-up."

"Well, I like it," she says softly. "I like the sound of it."

"I'd be happy to read you some poetry anytime," I say with what I hope is a genuine and not smarmy smile. "Or the NHL rules, if that would be more helpful to your current situation."

"I'm picking things up pretty quickly, though you're not wrong. I've never been on a pair of ice skates."

"How is that even possible?" I ask. "I think I skated before I could walk."

"I grew up in LA," she says drily.

"That's your excuse? There is an NHL team there, you know."

She makes an unimpressed noise. "I was more of a beach girl. I ran; I surfed; I played volleyball. Nothing required ice skates."

"Which of those put you through college?" I ask.

"Running."

"Cool, cool. Well, if you ever want an ice skating lesson, it would be my privilege to provide it to you."

"I just might take you up on that offer." A wicked grin spreads across her face. "If your bro-friend will spare you for a bit."

I'm ready to fire back a witty response, but she turns abruptly and gives me a small wave. "It was nice to meet you, Evan."

Watching her go, my mouth suddenly feels dry and my skin feels hot. It's a weird sensation, and I can feel it rushing throughout my body as the heat takes hold. Like spiking a fever in an icy room.

But it's no illness.

It's a bite.

I've been bitten, and the venom is in me now.

Far too late for me to do a thing about it.

FIVE

Holly

"I've started the favorite songs series," I say to Fiona as she hovers over my shoulder, looking at my laptop screen.

"Is it getting traffic?" she asks, disdain or disapproval dripping in her voice.

"A bit. But I haven't pushed the better-known players yet. I'm working my way up the ladder."

"Well don't drag it out if it's not driving traffic," she says. "Watch the analytics. Just pushing content without knowing its impact is not how we do things around here."

"I know," I say, trying to sound calm when I really want to tell her not to be a big jerk. "It will be good."

Fiona pushes her lips to one side, sniffs, and stands tall, smoothing the front of her dress and walking off without so much as another word. Yikes. Social media is on fire for this team, thank you very much. She needs to get the stick out of her butt and let me do my thing.

I continue working up the series. I had circulated a survey to the team, asking for lots of random information. I'm trying to link up a lot of our social media with the traditional media and advertising packages coming out of Fiona's advertising team office. As I review the newest package, I scan and find Evan's handsome face easily. God, he's painfully gorgeous.

This shouldn't be a thing, me crushing on one of our Crush players. Only a bazillion things could go wrong with having a thing for one of these guys, right? *Christ.* But he really is painfully hot. So hot. His dark hair is thick and a little on the long side right now. It was shorter when I started. It must grow fast. And he's always got stubble, like no matter if he shaves in the morning, the hair will just deposit itself right back on those sculpted cheeks.

Yum. He's yummy to look at.

And he was so cocky and flirtatious in person. Made me want to drop my panties, to be honest. But that's the problem, isn't it? There's probably a line of woman who drop their panties for a guy like him. I'd be some one-night-stand and it'd be awkward working with him afterward. Yeah, no thanks. I like this job.

At lunchtime, I head out into the afternoon sun, relishing the feel of warmth on my skin as I call my friend Pam. Pam was my roommate all through college. She's a spitfire blonde who always speaks her mind, sometimes when I'd rather she not. She's a physical therapist, which is pretty much perfect for her personality.

"What's up, hot stuff?" she asks. "How's Sin City treating you?"

"Well, I haven't seen much sin," I say.

"That's too bad. I'm seriously disappointed in you. You've been there, what, over a week now? No sin at all?"

"Ha. This is me we're talking about," I say.

"Yes, Miss Goody Two-Shoes." I can almost hear her eyes rolling. "You need to live a little. What have you been doing out there? Wait—let me guess. Running. Working. Laying out by the pool being an introvert."

I grin at the phone. "You got me. I have indeed been doing all of those things. Also ogling hot hockey players, though. I even flirted with one."

"What?" She sounds amused but genuinely shocked. "I love that. Which one? I'll look him up."

"Evan Kazmeirowicz," I say with a sigh. "So gorgeous. Panties practically fell off of their own free will when I was talking to him."

"Wow," she says. "Yep. Yep. I see that. Smoldering. Dark hair. Nice green eyes. Good stubble. That's a man, Holly. He's not some soccery-playing-wiener-boy like the last one. Nope. That's a big dude. Probably has a long—"

"Okay, okay," I interrupt quickly. "I can't be thinking about him like that. He's, like, a colleague. I can't sleep with colleagues."

"He's a dirty sports boy who probably doesn't even have any idea there are actual humans making the business side of the team work. He's probably dumb as a box of rocks."

I make a dubious noise. "I don't think so. He's cocky for sure, but in no way dumb."

"Well, he's worth a good dirty dream at the least. I approve of your ogling and lust. Nicely done, Holls."

"So, I'm actually calling to see if I can crash with you while the team is in LA for games later this month."

"Never a problem, but won't the Crush put you up in a hotel or something?" she asks. "They that cheap?"

"Oh, they would, but I'd have to share with another person and I'd much rather bunk with you. It'll give us a chance to catch up. I miss my roomie."

"Aww, I miss you too, and it's never a problem. Just text me the dates."

We chat a little more about her job and some guy she's been seeing before she turns the conversation back to Evan. "So, I think I've heard about this guy."

"Evan, really?"

"Yeah, remember Tony? The guy I dated a little last year?"

"I guess..."

"Well, he was a huge LA hockey fan and we went to a game against the Crush. I remember that last name coming up. He was new to the NHL, but Tony said he's like a scoring machine. Fast, lethal, totally focused on the game. But I guess he's got a bit of a reputation. He and his buddy...whatever the defenseman's name is. That guy's a big partier, sleeps around a lot."

"Wow, you do know things," I say. "Georg is the other guy. He does have a reputation around here. Jury's out on Kazmeirowicz."

"Well, be careful," she warns. "Guy like him will chew you up and spit you out. Though it might feel good to—"

"Nope. This conversation is over," I laugh back. "I'll send you those dates, Pammy."

We finish the call and I head back inside. I start doing some research on a Facebook series I want to develop and end up coming across a bunch of pictures of the players at special events. There are a lot of Evan. It looks like they tote him out as a poster boy to all kinds of charity and sponsor events. It makes sense. He's a natural in front of the press, very cocky but never saying anything that will cause the team any trouble. He looks good on camera, of course. But in the photos I find, there are always women at his side. Different women, never the same ones twice.

He's probably a total player. Which is not something I'm interested in. My friend Pam isn't wrong. I'm too much of a good girl for a guy like him. I only dated three guys all through college, including the one I got engaged to before I realized he was having a side gig with someone from the women's soccer team.

Yes, best just to shut the book on this little fangirl crush. Evan is way out of my league and I don't need the trouble a guy like him inevitably stirs up. It might be worth a one-night-stand, but...I am so not that kind of girl.

Forget it and move on. That's what I'm doing.

Reunited with my sense of self-preservation, I'm able to really focus on my work for the rest of the day. I power through some planning for all of our platforms before sending my suggested calendar to Fiona for a look-over. I won't say she's been unsupportive, because it's not the case. But she's sort of disconnected. She pops in periodically and seems unenthused with individual ideas, even though those ideas are part of a larger plan. I figure she just needs to see the grand vision and how it all fits together, both from platform to platform and also within the loftier branding plan.

"Butts in seats," she has said on numerous occasions. "Everything we do to promote this team, Holly, needs to be with the overarching idea of driving people to *want* to be in our stands."

I feel most people want to connect with their heroes. They want to feel like they really know them, and social media creates this illusion. So, we need not focus on their hockey stats, they're just one part of the plan. We should also allow small glimpses into who they are as people, as much as we can safely do without lying or disrupting their privacy.

When I leave for the day, my head is swirling with thoughts about my work. This is not a bad thing, but it's hard for me to wind down. I decide to go for a run to expel some energy.

Putting one foot in front of the other has always been my centering activity. No matter what was going on in my life, I could put in my earbuds, turn up a song with a good beat, and just run. So, after this productive day that's left my mind racing, I decide to lace up my shoes and take a long one. I run and run, probably seven miles, before I stop in my tracks gazing at a billboard featuring the faces of the Crush's top scorers. Of course, dead center, is the gorgeous Evan Kazmeirowicz.

"Ugh," I grunt to myself as I pull my water bottle from my running belt and take a swig. *Why's he got to be so beautiful?*

With work successfully out of my head, I spend the seven miles back home thinking about a certain winger with a deadly smile, and a head of hair I'd give anything to put my hands in.

SIX

EVAN

know, I know, my car is awesome. It should be, for a $400,000 Lamborghini Aventador. I like the way it comes off the tongue. Aventador.

It's white and fast and the V12 engine sounds like a mountain is about to come down on top of you. Especially in the parking garage at the arena as I rumble down several levels to the team's private parking area. I pull into my spot, next to Georg's candy-red Audi, and turn off my baby's purring engine. Georg is also into motorcycles, but his contract prohibits him riding during the season. He bitches about it, but the rule is there for a reason.

Can I just share I spent all of last night tossing and turning, thinking about the luscious lips on Holly Laurent? I normally don't spend a lot of time thinking about any one specific woman. Certainly not to the degree I've thought about her. Wonder why that is?

Either way, it left me feeling pent up and in need of some serious stress reduction, so I came in early to hit the gym before a meeting with my agent and the team's owner. With two goals in my first game, we're gearing up a discussion about a bonus for consistent performance. I've got a sweet deal, no complaints, but NHL teams fill seats by scoring, and by winning. I'm leading that charge and I don't see a thing wrong with setting up a little carrot for myself, just a little something to keep me motivated.

I start with a fast two-mile run on the treadmill and follow with a full body circuit for arms, core, and legs. Though Georg's car was in its spot, I don't see him, so I wonder where he is in the building.

My workout helps calm my overworked mind for sure, but my body is still spring, like a snake waiting to strike. I have a feeling whoever gets in my way on the ice next is going to regret it. *Look out, Mikhail.*

After a quick shower, I change into dress pants and a sharp button-down. Not too dressy but not too casual. Usually Scott Rose, my agent, is in a suit while Max Terry, the owner, will be in golf-wear. If he's in his suite for games, he's usually in a suit, looking slick, but on these days, he'll be gearing up to head out on the links.

I wander into the owner's suite and find both of them already there, enjoying Scotch on the rocks.

"Start the party without me, why don't you." I go in joking.

"Get you one?" Max asks.

"Nah, thanks, I just came from the gym."

"Good for you," he says. "We need you in tip-top shape if we're going to keep squeezing goals out of you."

"No squeezing necessary, I'm just doing what you pay me to do."

He laughs. "Yes, you sure are. Thank God someone is."

We all laugh, and Scott jumps into the conversation. "Well, since we're talking about this, I wanted to run something past you."

"What's that?" Max asks.

"Evan here is metrics driven," Scott says. "He's like the best guy on your sales force. He'll meet his numbers if you pay him well, but he'll triple his numbers if you dangle a little bonus in front of him."

Max lets a little, amused laugh out through his nose. "More money, huh? It's only game one. Long season ahead..."

Scott jumps in and the two banter about it, but in the end, Max Terry is no dummy. He knows I'm leading scorer in the Western Division. I led us straight into the playoffs last year and it was only a torn ligament that kept me off the ice for the final few games and All-Star series. Max brings this up, worried I'll push myself too hard, injure myself and cost us the playoffs again.

"The All-Star games are a goal of mine," I say. "If I don't make it to playoffs, I don't make it to All-Stars."

"Strange prioritization, but whatever motivates you," Max says. He brushes a hand through his silver hair. "Let me think about it, talk with Bellikowski about it."

We shoot the shit for a few more minutes before Max grumbles that he needs to get moving or he'll miss his tee time. We all walk out together. While Scott and Max head out to the parking garage, I stick around, saying I want to pop in on Fiona to talk about a media package she's been planning.

They must know that's bullshit. I never go into the administrative offices. Like, ever. But I really want to see if Holly is in. I just really feel the need to see her, which makes me the equivalent of a desperate teenager, but whatever.

I wander in, noting the wide eyes of some of the staff. Fiona comes out of her office, stiff backed like she's got a stick up her ass. Seriously, woman's kind of uptight. Anyway, she fusses over me with shit like, "Oh, Mr. Kazmeirowicz, what are you doing up here? How can we help you? It's such an honor to have one of our players visit the administrative suite."

"I was actually looking for—"

Bud Bellikowski, the GM, comes out, from under a rock somewhere I suspect, his tie askew, his thinning hair wind-blown. "I thought I heard one of our big stars was in the house," he says, his hands up like he's trying to raise the roof.

I'm sure my placating smile probably just looks uncomfortable. "I just popped in from another meeting with

Max," I say. "Thought I might have a conversation with the new social media guru."

"Why?" Fiona asks quickly. "Has she upset you somehow? The Kazochev thing?"

I shake my head, chuckling. "No, no, I'm not upset. It's funny and getting a lot of traffic. Now, I just wanted to check in with an idea, and an offer. Is her workspace around here?"

Fiona looks like she just tasted something sour. She looks toward a cubicle which is, unfortunately, empty of the woman I'm itching to see. "Looks like she's stepped out," she says. "Can I give her a message for you?"

"No ma'am," I say. "I'll just leave her a note to give me a call."

"Hhhmpf," is Fiona's answer. She opens her mouth then shuts it again, folding her arms across her chest.

"Is something wrong?" I ask.

"I'm sure you're aware," she says, tight-lipped, "we have a strict policy here about fraternization."

I lift my eyes to meet hers, a challenge there. "Well, I'm under a pretty nicely-worded contract for the next couple of years which doesn't say a thing about it."

"She's not, however," Fiona says. "I mean, I suppose the two of you can do whatever hobnobbing you want, but I doubt you want the young lady to lose her job, since you like her work so much."

The words she says, they make sense. No, I don't want Holly to lose her job. She does seem to be pretty good at it. Great, actually. But the venom, the threat embedded there...I don't like being threatened.

I narrow my eyes at her. "I'll leave a note for her. I expect it to remain private. I can assure you there will be no...fraternization."

"Good, fine," she says, waving a hand at me like she's bored with the conversation. "I appreciate your interest in our little media operation."

She wanders back toward her office. Bud is still standing around, looking totally lost.

"You okay, there, Bud?" I ask.

"That woman scares the shit out of me," he says.

"You and me both, buddy. Hey, you think it would be okay for me to teach young Holly how to skate? I think it's a damn shame that our social media genius has never been on a pair of blades. Not fraternizing or whatever, just part of her training. Her uncle Troy's one of our top scouts; I'm shocked he never took her to a game and I think it would really help her understanding of the game to get out on the ice."

"Oh, yeah," I'm sure it'll be fine," he says. "Don't worry about it."

"Great, buddy, thanks," I say, smacking him on the back.

"Yeah, yeah, okay, Evan," he mumbles. Then he shakes his head and bumbles back toward whatever hallway or tunnel he came from.

I find a notepad and a pen and jot down a message.

Holly,

Nice to meet you post-game the other night. Love what you're doing with the team's social this season. Real creative stuff, but I think it could only be enhanced if you actually knew how to ice skate. I'd like to personally oversee your training in this area. Join me for a skate at the Cosmo? Number is 777-857-7933. Text or call and we'll set up a lesson.

Best,

Evan

I head out of the office, whistling as I walk, head held high like the cockstrong young buck I am. My cell rings as I get into my car.

"Yo, Georgie."

"I saw your clip with Kacey King. The woman is still hot for you, my man. Did you tap that again?"

"Nah," I say. "Not interested."

"What? Are you nuts? She's blazing hot."

"Yeah, she's all right. Not as great in the sack as you might think. Not worth a second go."

"More than once means feelings," Georg says, trying to imitate my accent.

"For her," I say. "Not for me."

He laughs. "Were you in the gym?"

"Earlier, yes," I say. "Then in a meeting with my agent."

I decide not to mention I went looking for Holly. Somehow, for some reason, I don't want Georg thinking about Holly like she's just some chick I want to bang. I'm not sure what she is to me yet, and I guess I'd rather have the idea of her to myself for the moment.

We have the day off since yesterday was a game day, but we'll have to be back on ice again tomorrow, plus we have some PSA's to shoot for the charitable foundation the team runs. It will be a busy day, a day that will keep me away from my phone for most of it.

It's been a long time since I've had to wait around for a girl to call me. Normally, I see what I want, I make it known I want it, and it appears. But Holly Laurent? No, I'm pretty sure that's not how this young woman operates.

I knew it when I saw her the first day in the arena. I felt something crackle between us and call me cheesy, but it was like it was chemistry or something. And now I'm sitting here with my dick in my hand, waiting for her to call as if I'm some teenage kid who asked a girl to prom.

As I drive, the song *Limelight* by Rush comes on the radio. I am a real hockey guy like that, loving the old rock songs. So I turn it up and let it wash over me, not even a little bit sure what the heck Holly Laurent is already doing to me.

SEVEN

Holly

Everyone is looking at me funny as I walk back into the office suite. What, do I have mustard on my shirt or something? I mean, I grabbed a hot dog from a food truck outside while I was walking and talking to Pam...

I run into the ladies' room and check—nope, no mustard. Nothing in the teeth. Overall, I look pretty okay, so what's with the strange side-eye action?

Whatever. I wander back to my cubicle and call Troy. He's about to head out on the road to scout minor league players and I want to catch him before he gets too busy.

"Hey Holly dolly, how's my favorite niece?"

"Heya," I say. "Your *only* niece just wanted to check in before you head out on the road."

"Yep," he says. "You good? Everything going okay?"

"All is well. Thanks again for helping me connect here. I wasn't sure if I'd enjoy it, but I really do. It's been a blast so far."

"Well, you're really killing it, from what I can tell," he says. "I'm loving the creativity on the social sites."

"Thanks. I'm not sure my boss is into it, but she hasn't stopped me so far."

"Best to ask forgiveness rather than permission," Troy says with a little chuckle. "She's been around a while, probably doesn't even know a thing about social media. You heard from your daddy lately?"

"Not in the past week or two. He said he was tied up in business."

"Standard bullshit out of him, then," Troy says, his voice full of contempt. "I love my brother, but he needs to get his head out of his ass."

"Well, thankfully for me, I have you."

"I'm no substitute for the real thing," he says, "but I'm always here. I'll call you from the road when I can."

"Okay. Have a good trip, Uncle Troy. Love ya."

We hang up and I sit for a minute, willing myself to not cry. I'm not usually emotional about my parents. They've been divorced since I was in middle school. My dad always traveled a lot for his big oil job, and when they split up, he moved to the Middle East. He rarely comes to the States anymore, and I hear from him on birthdays and Christmas, with a few sparing phone calls in between.

My mom remarried when I was a sophomore in high school. She spent my last three years at home traveling back and forth between Europe and Los Angeles, because her husband owns a multi-national company based in France. Once I went to college, they set up a trust fund, sold the house, and moved overseas full time.

So while I'm not technically an orphan, I feel like one sometimes. And Uncle Troy has been kind of a surrogate parent for me, always there when I have needed someone. Moving to Las Vegas has been good for me, but everything still feels really new. It doesn't feel like home yet. I'm trying not to be emotional about it, but for whatever reason, I'm really homesick for LA today.

Of course, I'm not one to wallow so I flip open my laptop, surprised to find a piece of paper there.

Oh my God, it's a note. A hand-written note. From Evan Kazmeirowicz.

I read it three times, feeling my face heat. And other parts, too, for that matter. My nipples literally strain against my bra as I think if him, standing here at my cubicle, slipping this note into my computer. Oh. My. God.

I pop up to my feet and look across the station to one of my coworkers, Carly, who handles media passes. She looks up from her screen.

"What's wrong with you?" she asks. "Your cheeks are all pink. You sick?"

"No," I whisper. "Did—was—did someone come looking for me earlier?"

"You mean someone hot and green-eyed and dark-haired?" she asks, smirking.

"Yes!" I hiss.

"Yes, a person matching that description came looking for you."

"Why?" I practically screech.

"He said he had an idea to run past you. Fiona about blew a gasket. Started going on about the fraternization clause in our contracts."

"Oh shit," I say, cringing. "I wonder if he's pissed about the Kazochev thing?"

"Didn't seem like it," she says with a shrug. "He said he thought it was funny."

"No wonder everyone looked at me like I had seven heads," I say. "Holy cow. Okay. Thanks."

She nods and goes back to her work and I sit down, trying to catch my breath. Evan was here. Looking for me. He wants to take me ice skating.

Is 'ice skating' code for naked bed dancing? Because I think I'd be down for that, if that's what it meant.

No. No. I'm not a slut and it's a slutty, slutty thought. I won't be one of Evan's many bed partners. I won't just spread my legs for his wicked, wicked tongue and his surely very talented fingers and his big, long—

Nope. Stop it. Control yourself, Holly Laurent. You are a professional. He is a professional. You can surely enjoy his company and learn to ice skate without it ending in hot, multi-orgasmic sex. Right? Right.

I bumble through the rest of my day, totally unable to focus thanks to the note that's burning a hole in my pocket. Do I call him? Just go skating, leave it friendly and professional? No, no, I can't. Fiona would fire me in a heartbeat for fraternizing with a player like that. And I like my job. My job is worth more than a one-night stand...even if the one-night stand is with someone as achingly beautiful as Evan.

Bud Bellikowski, our GM, comes over around four-thirty. "Hey, you ready to grab a bite? Talk shop?"

Oh, crap. I forgot we set up time to go grab an early dinner and talk about my performance so far.

"Sure," I say. "Let me just save this file and we can go."

I finish up and shut down my computer, grabbing my purse and following Bud as he shuffles toward the doors. Fiona pops her head out of her office as we pass, giving me a questioning look. I make a face that I hope looks like—*Hey, I have no idea; I'm just going with the flow.*

We head down and out of the arena to a restaurant about a block away. It's just a little pub-type of place, fairly quiet and not flashy—rare for Las Vegas. Bud orders a Michelob Lite—yuck—and I get seltzer water with lime. No way am I drinking in front of the GM.

"So..." Bud starts. He trails off and a placid smile remains on his face.

He's forgotten my name. I resist the urge to roll my eyes. Nothing like setting up a meeting with an employee whose name you can't remember.

"Holly," I say.

"Right, sorry," he says, his face turning red. "It's been a long day."

I nod. "Sure has."

"You missed Evan today," he says. "He came to talk with you about some ideas he had for social media."

"I heard."

"He also thinks anyone working for the team should know how to skate. He'd like to help you learn," Bud says. "We have a rule about fraternization among staff, but I've given him the okay, since he feels it would be valuable for you to have a feel for the ice, you know, in order to better represent the game."

I nearly snort at this but manage to keep what I think is a mostly-straight face. "Yes, sir," I say, trying not to laugh. "I'm sure Evan Kazmeirowicz feels very invested in making sure Crush employees have a good feel for the game."

Thankfully, he misses the sarcasm in my statement and just nods. "Well, then, it's settled. Let me know how your training goes."

"Sure will," I say. Though I'm certainly now back to thinking about being alone with Evan and wondering just how much detail I would need to share about our, ahem, training. No way am I accepting that invitation. No freaking way.

"So I also told Fiona I want you to get more video on those..." he stops, searching for the words again.

"Channels?" I ask. "Social media channels?"

"Yes!" he says, taking a swig of his beer. "Get together with them over there in video and see if we can get more live stuff into your work. Not just static photos."

"Sure, I can get with the video department to embed some video. I can also make live videos and interviews from my cell phone, especially on the road."

"Great, sounds good, Hillary," Bud says.

"It's Holly," I say.

"Sorry, yes," he says, shaking his head. He takes another swig of beer. "Long day."

We chat for a few minutes about the travel schedule.

"Am I supposed to go on the road for all of the away games, sir?" I ask. "I know I'll do the California tour, but do I always travel with the team?"

"Yes, yes," Bud says. "Fiona's team always travels with the boys on their road games. It's an exhausting schedule, I know, but she likes for us to be present for the media as much as possible."

Bud finishes his beer and looks at his watch. "Well, I'd better get on home to the missus," he says. "Good chat, Hallie. I'll see you in the morning. Good job you're doing. Real good. More video."

He scoots out of the booth and toddles off, leaving me to pay the bill.

"Thank God he likes cheap beer," I say, looking at the bill and tossing my credit card down.

While I wait for the waitress to bring back my card, I pull out the note from Evan and read it again. I type him a quick text. Evan replies almost instantly.

Holly: Thanks for the note and offer, but I can't accept.

Evan: Why not? You've never been skating. I think you should try it out.

Holly: I will, but I can't fraternize with a player.

Evan: Oh that. Bellikowski cleared it.

Holly: I know. Still. Fiona's a stickler.

Evan: She doesn't own me.

Holly: But she does, kind of, own me. She's my boss.

Evan: Well, I promise I'll keep it totally professional. Scout's honor.

Holly: Sorry, Evan. Sounds fun but I just started my job here and I really like it. I can't risk it.

He doesn't reply after that and I'm sure I've made him upset. He's probably not used to women turning him down. And to be honest, I didn't want to turn him down. I just can't start something with him. It's bound to go nowhere and if we slept together, I'm sure it would be awkward after.

I think about it for a long time. Did I make the right decision? I'm sure I did. But do I wish I hadn't?

Yep. Pretty much.

EIGHT

EVAN

Scott and I are grabbing lunch in the pub by the arena. I'm in workout clothes because I came in for a clear-the-head gym workout first, and I have practice right after.

He's, of course, in an impeccable suit. His short, brown hair has just a few strands of grey at the temples. He's probably fortyish, a total bull when it comes to representing his players.

"So Bellikowski cleared a path for incentives," Scott's saying. "Which, you knew he would because he's easy like that."

"He is," I say, distracted.

"I think we can set up lines of income based on scoring, assists, All-Star participation, vote to Team Captain," he says as he shoves French fries in his mouth.

I pick at my sandwich and try to pay attention. Honestly, though, my head just keeps going right back to Holly Laurent. I can't stop thinking about her, especially since I had that little text exchange with her. Where she turned me down.

I don't think I've been turned down by a woman since I was in, like, primary school.

"Hey, earth to Evan. You hearing me?"

"Huh?" I ask, coming back to reality. "What? Sorry."

"You okay, man?" he asks. "I know you took that hit in the first game. You concussed? Should we have forced protocol?"

"Oh, no," I say. "No, I'm totally fine."

"You're a star, Evan. We need you healthy. It's only September and the season is long. Let's get you checked out before you head out on the road, just to be safe. We can keep it quiet. No need to sound an alarm...just a quick check-up."

"No, it's cool, man," I say, putting up my hands. "I'm fine. Just a little zoned out today."

"I saw the glazed look you had out there after it happened," Scott says. "Everyone saw it on the big boards. Twitter was ablaze with commentary about you getting your egg cracked. Just go see the team doc, have him take a look. Do it as a favor to me, your old pal Scott, who is trying to get you even bigger money than the last big money I got you."

I shake my head and grin. "So what do you think about the rookie line this year?"

"You changing the subject on me, boy?" he asks, dipping three fries in ketchup and shoving in another mouthful.

"Yes, because I'm not concussed and I'm ready to talk about something else."

"Well what do you want to talk about?" he asks. "Because you sure as hell weren't interested in talking about money and incentives."

"Fair enough, I guess I deserved that."

"How's old Georg holding up so far?" he asks, granting me my subject change now that I've admitted I wasn't paying attention.

"He's Georg," I say with a shrug. "Ballsy, always at my side. Mostly sober."

This earns me a raised eyebrow and dubious snort from my agent.

"Okay, mostly sober while on the ice," I amend.

"I'll tell you," Scott says. "You two are a dream team most games. I'd love to take him on but he's a risk."

I shrug. "He likes women, partying, and hockey."

"In that order, unfortunately," Scott says. "He's too wild for me."

"He performs when we need him to, though. He hasn't played NHL that long. I'm sure he'll settle down."

"He's not a kid," Scott says. "If he was going to settle down, he would've already, so don't give me that line of horseshit. I know he wants representation, but I can't take on a risky bet like that. If he cleans up and keeps performing, I'll think about it."

"Well, you'll never convince him that women are a risk," I say.

"I'm not talking about women," he says. "If I was, you wouldn't have representation either. I'm talking about the fact his liver's probably going to defect back to Russia if he keeps it up. He needs to pick a healthier vice."

"Yeah," I say. "I mean, I'm not his babysitter."

"No," Scott says, "But you're his friend and his teammate."

I stew on this while I eat a bit of my lunch. I expect a hard practice, so I really should be getting something into my stomach for fuel.

"You asked about the rookie line," Scott says. "I think they look good so far. That kid you butt heads with seems like a wildcard."

"Kid's got a big chip on his shoulder," I say. "He's so young. Too young, probably. Should've played minors or nationals or something first. Or gone to college and played. He's out there thinking he's got to make his mark immediately. Doesn't want to be told shit. You know how it goes."

He nods. "I do know how it goes. I've signed plenty of kids his age. They're all the same. Stars in their eyes, money they've never seen before. Well, he's got talent, I'll give him that. He could probably use a good mentor."

"I'll assign Georg," I say with an eye roll.

"You'll assign you," he says. "Because you want to be Team Captain next year. Dumbass."

We move on, talking about Scott's wife and kids. His wife is a teacher and his kids are both in middle school. He beams while he talks about his family, as always, and I find I envy him for it. He obviously loves being a family man, a dad, a husband. I've never seen myself that way. In fact, I've actively driven the opposite direction of any kind of commitment thus far. But he makes it look not half bad.

He gets a phone call and says he has to take it. He mouths, "Go to the doctor," before tossing two twenties on the table and heading out, his voice getting louder as he bickers with someone about another athlete's contract.

I finish my sandwich, pay, and then head back out. I think about heading to the administrative offices but then change my mind. I don't want to look desperate. But maybe I could call...just leave a message. She's probably not going to answer during the workday anyway.

So, I dial Holly's number and when she picks up on the first ring, I find myself surprised enough that I don't really have anything planned to say.

"Hi, uh, Holly...it's Evan," I stammer. Like a fourteen-year-old, nervous kid. What the hell is wrong with me?

"I know," she says. "How can I help you?"

"Oh," I say, at a loss. She sounds very...professional. "Well, I called to follow up on our text exchange."

"You did, did you?" she asks.

"Yes, I wanted to let you know I really think you're missing out on a great opportunity. I've literally been on skates since I was a wee little thing. I'd be a bloody good teacher."

She lets out a little huff of a laugh. "Well."

"Well, what?"

44

"Well, your accent," she says. "The offer does sound better when it comes out like that. In writing, you sound American."

I laugh. "Well, thank the saints for a European accent. Is that a yes?"

"It's still a no, I'm afraid," she says apologetically. "I still need to eat, and my paycheck allows me to do that."

"What if I could guarantee you wouldn't lose your job?" I ask.

"Because you're God? Or a secret owner of the Crush? How could you possibly guarantee it?"

"You are quite feisty," I say. "I like it. And no, I am not God, though I have been called that name before."

"I assume this is your way of telling me you're good in bed," she shoots back. "Not the way to my heart, hearing about your other conquests."

I laugh out loud at this. "Well, I do understand that. But no, I was actually thinking of my teammates, who call me that when I score more than a hat trick in a game."

"Ah," she says. "A hat trick is three goals, right?"

"Right, and I could teach you all about it and more if you agree to a skating lesson with me. We'll totally focus on the game. And I give you my word I will be a perfect professional and gentleman."

"What about Fiona?"

"Fiona already heard my opinion on this matter, and Bud approved it right in front of her. He outranks her, and I could have her fired tomorrow if I really wanted it."

"You have that much power over the back office?" she asks incredulously.

"Well...actually...I don't know. But I know I covered this with both of them already. We're golden. I promise."

She laughs. "You drive a hard bargain. Let me think about it."

"So, it's not a hard no, then."

"It's not a hard no. Now let me get back to work before I really do get fired."

"Okay, bye for now, Holly."

"Bye, Evan," she says softly before she ends the call.

Okay. I feel better now. I can go to practice and bash some rookie heads and not be distracted by the one who nearly got away.

NINE

Holly

"**T**hat was really fun," I say as I follow Evan into his penthouse apartment. Of course, he lives in a long-term rental section of a big casino resort. He's a total baller like that.

His place is spacious with smooth leather furniture and hard-wood floors. The living room has floor-to-ceiling windows that look out over the lights of the Strip. It's stunning, really, and I stand there for a long time just watching the twinkling lights.

Evan's presence beside me creates a crackling chemistry that feels palpable. It makes my heart skip a beat, just like my heart skipped a beat every time our eyes met while we were at the skating rink. I shouldn't be here. I shouldn't have come up. The invitation was heavy with sexual tension because every time we touched on the ice, it felt like I might combust.

"This is really beautiful," I say. "This view."

"It never gets old," he says.

"My view is of a fenced-in, postage-stamp-sized backyard on one side, and a row of condos that look just like mine on the other." I don't know why I even offer the information it sounds so lame.

"Well, home is wherever you hang your hat." I sense he has moved right behind me.

I turn to look at him, to maybe make a joke about an old-fashioned saying, but instead, his face is right there, so close, and his lips are—

"I've wanted to kiss you all night," he says, leaning in close so I can feel his lips move against my ear. "The way your cheeks looked in the ice rink, so pink. And your eyes were so bright. I've never wanted to kiss someone more."

I can barely get real words out, but I manage, "So do it."

And he does. His beard is softer than I'd expect as his lips brush against mine. The kiss is soft, tentative, but my body wants more, so I open to him as his hands find my face. My arms wrap around his waist, my hands find their way up his shirt, my skin on his skin.

His tongue flicks against my bottom lip, an invitation I accept, opening my mouth, sighing loudly.

We move, still kissing, falling onto the soft leather couch, him between my legs. His hands roam, pushing my sweater up. I pull it hastily over my head and find him just as eager, his teeth nipping at my nipples through my thin, lace bra.

My hands push at his shirt, fumbling as I work the buttons, pushing it away from his chest. I think I gasp a little as I take in the panels of his stomach, the definition of his pectorals. I run my hands over his skin, over the hair on his chest that dissolves into a happy trail down beneath his jeans.

My explorations continue as I cup between his legs, feeling the hardness of him, contained neatly by his pants. "I want them off," I breathe, "I want to feel you."

We both work our pants down our legs, then our underwear. But while I'm ready, ready for him, he disappears, sliding down the length of me, his face finding the apex between my thighs, his tongue lapping at the already-wet folds there. He finds my aching, swollen clit and flicks it with his tongue as his fingers find my entrance and sink inside.

My back arches and I moan something indecipherable. He knows what he's doing, that Evan, every motion of his tongue, his fingers, pushing me up a cliff wall. I can see the top. I know I'll fall over the edge soon, into some abyss.

"Come for me, Holly," he says.

And there it is. The sensation of falling. Of not breathing. Of forgetting my own name. My body tingles as the waves come.

I blink a few times as the ecstasy subsides, unsure for a moment what planet I'm even on. Evan moves up my body, kissing at my stomach, the underside of my breasts. When his mouth closes over mine, I taste sweetness and musk and his beard wet with my arousal.

He slides inside of me, a perfect fit that makes me cry out, my hips flexing toward him as he begins to move. My hands find his bare ass, my fingernails dig into his skin, driving him forward, faster and faster.

He never stops kissing me as he moves. Our tongues swirl together and I only break away to breathe, so he puts his mouth on my neck. My breasts rub against his chest, my nipples so hard they ache.

I feel myself inching closer, closer, and when he tells me to let go, he lets go, too. He roars his pleasure as I soar once again, my pussy tight around his cock, my clit pulsing in gripping spasms.

When he collapses on top of me, his head on my bare breasts, I reach up and stroke that dark, soft hair of his.

This feels right. I hardly know him, but this feels right, and...

I wake up with a start, sitting straight up in bed. Oh my God. I just had the hottest, sexiest dream about Evan Kazmeirowicz. It felt so real. Real enough that I absolutely ache between the legs, my abdomen heavy with desire, my underwear soaked.

I guess it has been a while. I haven't been with a man since my ex-fiancé. The one who cheated on me.

Time for a hot shower. I trudge to the bathroom, turning on the water and stepping out of my pajamas. Thank God for the massage mode on the shower head, makes it much easier for a girl to get off in a pinch.

I'm so embarrassed. I can't believe I had such a dirty, dirty dream about a player. I swear I already told myself I wasn't going to go there with him. No way. He's a total player and even if it was as good as all that, it would only be a one-time thing, and then I'd feel crummy about myself, and it would be all weird at work, and I'd probably lose my job, and, and, and—

See? Not a good idea.

I decide to text Pam. She's always good at helping me through these peculiar situations.

Holly: Pammy-jammy!! Holy cow. I just had a HOT sex dream about hot hockey player. Help!

Pam: Details.

Holly: No way. Just very hot.

Pam: Make it real, my child.

Holly: Can't if I want to keep my job.

Pam: You're killing me with this.

Holly: I'm killing you? You're not the one who woke up in need of an immediate trip to vibrator-land.

Pam: No need for vibrator if you just sex the guy up. You know he wants you. Unless the invitation to learn to skate was, like, just an invitation to learn to skate.

Holly: No. I'm sure it was just a ploy to get into my panties. And he's a player. I saw him flirting with the blonde from local TV station, so...

Pam: Whatever. You know you need a good romp. Just go, get off, and move on. Don't make a thing of it.

Holly: When have I ever just gone and gotten off?

Pam: True. But you can always start now. Go!

Holly: No way. I have morals.

Pam: Ugh. Goody two-shoes.

Holly: Says the girl who has yet to officially lose her v card.

Pam: A technicality really. I know stuff. Changing subject now. Are you still coming this way?

Holly: Yup. I'll try to get you a pass so you can sit with me for the game.

Pam: Yippee! Will there be mullets? I won't come if there are no mullets.

Holly: There are a few mullets, yes...

Pam: Woohoo!

Holly: Maybe I should do an Instagram series on Hockey Hair?

Pam: YASS!

Pam and I go back and forth with all kinds of ideas for different social media series I could do, and while some are really stupid, others are actually pretty good. I write in my journal as we text, and when we finish our conversation, I genuinely feel better.

I can do this. It was only a dream. I do not have to allow myself to get wrapped up in this guy. Just because he's super-hot, and super successful, and seemingly not a total jerkwad, does not mean that I should just drop my pants and let him have his way.

Like some animal.

Like some, hot, wild, primal male...

Ugh. I'm taking another shower.

TEN

EVAN

There are tits and ass everywhere I look. And legs, lots of legs. Georg and three of our teammates talked me into a trip into the city tonight. We're playing in New Jersey tomorrow night, and even though I specifically said no—three separate times—he wore me down and now, here we are.

"Don't you remember the days," Georg muses as he tips his vodka on the rocks to his lips.

"I remember lots of days, buddy," I say. "Be more specific."

"Sochi," he says, slurring a little. "Babes, late nights, games played on two hours of sleep after lots of drinks and sex we couldn't even remember the next day."

"You couldn't remember," I say. "I remembered just fine because I wasn't blackout drunk."

"*Perdoon stary,*" Georg says with a burp and a laugh.

"Yeah, yeah," I say with an eye roll. "Call me an old fart."

"What about that hot blonde television reporter?" Georg says. "She wants you. You've had her before. Take her again."

"Take her? I'm not a caveman."

"Oh I forget, you are such a gentleman," Georg says. The other guys laugh.

"Okay, so I'm not," I say with a shrug. "I still don't want Kacey. Already been there, brother. You think she's so hot, you take a shot."

The music picks up and the lights go low. A dancer comes out, so our attention goes to the show on stage. Georg and the other guys are all drop-jaw, making hooting sounds, throwing money up on the stage. The woman is gorgeous, tits totally fake, with long, red hair. She's very fit, with good abs and shapely legs. She's a good performer, too, a good dancer. I throw a twenty on stage, just to show my appreciation.

"Well now," Georg eggs me on, "about time you get into the show a little."

"I appreciate her artistry," I say, grinning.

"I appreciate her tits," Georg says. "but I would more appreciate her twat in my face."

"I don't think this is that kind of place," I say.

"We'll put our twats in your face," a girlish voice says.

We turn and find three women behind us. They're youngish, early twenties, and all dressed scantily with cleavage bared. Georg grins like a wolf when one says, "Don't you all play for the Crush?"

"Are you hockey fans?" one of the guys asks.

"We are!" the tiny one with short dark hair says as she jumps up and down.

Great, puck bunnies. How the hell did they find us in a strip club in Manhattan?

Georg pulls her onto his lap and she giggles, pulling out her phone so they can take pictures together. She pulls out a Sharpie and has him and the other guys all sign her breast with it. I shake my head when she tries to hand me the pen. She makes a pouty face that turns back into a smile when Georg whispers something in her ear. Likely, it's something derogatory about me, but I don't care.

Another of the girls goes to hang with the other guys, but the third, a dark-haired girl with a tiny waist, sits on my lap.

"I'm not really into this," I say. "I'm sorry. Nothing personal."

"Gay?" she asks with a giggle.

"No, definitely not."

"Taken?"

"Nope," I say, taking a swig of my beer.

"Well, then, why not take what's being offered?" she asks.

"I've got a game tomorrow. Superstitious," I lie.

"Okay, well, at least take a selfie with me?"

"I guess I can do that." I cave to her request, determined to blow this shit show the minute she's off my lap.

She holds her phone out to take the picture but right before she captures the image of us, she grabs my hand and slaps it onto her boob. She snaps the picture before I can even pull my hand away.

"Come on," I say. "Delete that."

She giggles and hops up, running over to my teammates. All of the girls take pictures before they finally take off, saying they'll be at the game tomorrow.

I shake my head, knowing those pictures will be all over social media by night's end. I kind of want to call Holly just to tell her it was a non-sanctioned boob grab, but I stop myself. My annoyance must be all over my face, though, because a wandering stripper comes over and asks if I need a "pick-me-up."

"What's that?" I ask.

"Dealer's choice," she says. "Lap dance out here for twenty. Private dance for fifty. You can touch for a hundred."

"I'm good," I tell her, "but thanks."

She shimmies all around me. "I'd let you touch for free, big guy."

"No thank you. Go see my friend over there, the guy with the long hair."

"Suit yourself," she says, heading over to Georg, who is glad to slip a twenty in the waistband of her tiny thong knickers.

I stand up and lean over their little lap-dance situation. "I'm heading back to the hotel, calling it a night."

"*Ti durak*," he says cheerfully.

"Yes, I'm a moron," I say. "As always, don't do anything I wouldn't do. And don't end up in the hospital. I need you on the ice tomorrow, fuckwad."

He waves me off and I shove my hands in my pockets as I make my way for the door, calling for a car service to come get me and take me back across the bridge. Holly came on this trip. Maybe I should see what she's up to. Maybe warn her about the titty-grab picture. She'd probably want a heads up, right? That there's likely something potentially negative coming on social media?

I decide to text her as I sit in the back of the car.

Evan: Fair warning. I was accosted by a fan and she made me touch her boob. It'll probably be on social media soon.

Holly: Hello to you, too.

Evan: Sorry. Hello. And sorry in advance. I did not initiate the boob-grab. I was assaulted.

Holly: You are a grown man. You may grab a boob if you wish, as long as it was desired and consensual.

Evan: Why are you always so cool and practical?

Holly: Why are you telling me about a boob-grab picture?

Evan: Thought it might affect your social media work.

Holly: Where is the eye-roll emoji?

Evan: Okay. Well, don't say I didn't warn you.

Holly: I will shield my innocent eyes from such images of debauchery. Where did said boob-grab photo occur, may I ask?

Evan: Err...

Holly: House of sin?

Evan: Pretty much. Strip club in the city. Not my idea.

Holly: Let me guess, you were accosted and forced to drive into the city to look at half-naked women against your will?

Evan: Yes, that.

Holly: Well, at least your story is consistent.

Evan: What are you doing right now?

Holly: Texting you. Watching Chopped.

Evan: Want to skinny-dip in the hotel pool when I get back?

Holly: Pass.

Evan: Want to meet me at Rockefeller Center for ice skating?

Holly: Tempting but no.

Evan: Where is the crying emoji?

Holly: You're not crying. You're too busy looking at naked women.

Evan: I am in a vehicle, alone, on my way back to the hotel. Honest engine.

Holly: Who says honest engine?

Evan: Scout's honor?

Holly: LOL. You're no boy scout. Goodnight, Evan.

Evan: Goodnight, Holly.

Damn. Thwarted again. That woman has self-control like no one I have ever met before.

I'm going to have to up my game with her.

ELEVEN

HOLLY

So, because I'm a glutton for punishment, I immediately open up social media. And, yep, there's the aforementioned boob-grab picture, complete with tags to the team. Thankfully, I've set it up so I can un-tag photos which are deemed inappropriate. I do just that, though I can't do anything about the hashtags that put the photo into the mix of photos I have previously approved and placed on purpose.

I scan the picture. I can see Georg's hair just off to the side, but the focus is definitely on Evan and this fangirl, her long hair silky around her shoulders, his hand copping a feel of her ample breast. He's smiling, and it doesn't look forced.

See? This is why I can't give in to this guy. He was out at a strip club, paying women to dance naked for him. He willingly put his hand on another woman's breast for a photo-op. It just doesn't sit well with me. And he just casually mentioned it in a text, acting like it was totally on the woman, like he had nothing to do with it.

But here's the rub: I can Google him and find countless other like-type photos. Evan likes the attention, has since well before he ever joined the Crush. This is just who he is—a slobbering, boob-grabbing pig who likes to have his way with women and then jettison them off into nowhere, as if they never existed. There's even a blog online where women talk about sex with hockey players. Evan is mentioned more than once, and always as a player. I need none of that in my life right now. I think I will stick to dream-Evan, and the untold pleasures of my massaging shower-head.

I must keep my work life separate from my personal life. I mean, not that I have much of a personal life to speak of. It's been really hard to meet people in Las Vegas. My coworkers are nice, but they don't really socialize much, maybe because of the weird fraternization policy, and while I've met a few of my neighbors, no one has struck me as friend material yet. And forget meeting men. Not that I want to. Not really.

On the plane out to New Jersey, the whole team, the coaching and training staff, and the media team were all on board. It was fun. I enjoyed the camaraderie of having a work team, and the excitement of heading out on our first away-stretch was really special. I do love my job.

I'm not angry with Evan. I mean, he is who he is, and he was that person long before he took an interest in me. But I won't let myself believe his interest is in anything other than a quick interlude, sex without strings. And I'm just not that girl.

I type one line of text to him before turning off the light and trying to sleep: **I'm not the girl for you.**

We're doing three away games in a row, starting in New Jersey, then to New York, and finally Philadelphia. During the New Jersey game, I'm on my phone and laptop simultaneously, live-tweeting the game and running promos on the other channels throughout the whole thing. We're getting a lot of engagement, which is awesome, and whenever we score people become all riled up online. The game is also really exciting. I don't know why I didn't realize how exciting hockey can be. Hockey moves very fast, and I'm finally starting to understand the basic rules. Evan and Georg both get sent to the penalty box at the same time so watching the team rally while New Jersey is on a power play becomes a nail-biting scenario.

There's a big fight at the end of the second period, where one of the New Jersey players takes a swing at one of our rookie players. The kid's tooth flies out of his mouth, a moment that gets replayed on the JumboTron about fourteen times. The crowd loves it and the kid seems none the worse for the wear, so I shoot out a few short videos of the incident, getting almost instant feedback from our fans. They are somewhat bloodthirsty, but I guess many hockey fans are.

Fiona has a press conference set up after the game and, of course, Evan is at the center of it, along with David Chalamet, and the rookie Mikhail. Evan scored a hat trick in the first period, while David and Mikhail paired up for scores and assists on two more goals in the third. It was a pretty spectacular win for the Crush, and the press is pretty amped up as they fire questions at the guys.

Everything goes fine, for the most past, though the rookie is salty throughout the whole thing, making a comment about some players being puck-hogs, and how he appreciates that the Team Captain is a mentor and team player. Even I can tell, from where I sit at the back of the room, Evan has to use all the self-control he has to keep from responding to the underhanded attack. The reality is it's Mikhail who hogs the puck, but his shots on goal are wild and uncontrolled. He certainly lacks the finesse of Evan and Georg, who both work well together.

David says something totally diplomatic about it being great to have such diverse talent on the team, diffusing things before anyone can make more stupid comments on the record. Evan looks relieved and relaxed, but Mikhail looks ready to attack at any moment. The press can sense it, and one asks if the winning streak can continue with such obvious animosity on the team. David easily diverts this one, too, and Fiona steps in quickly, saying that the team needs to get going. She shoos the reporters out and the three players head back to the locker rooms.

When everyone is out of earshot, Fiona grabs my arm. "That rookie is going to be the death of me," she says.

"Why put him on camera?" I ask.

"We need young blood on camera. He's a hard worker. Fans like him.," she says. She sighs and puts her hands on her hips. "This is Chalamet's last season, and he's a total diplomat. Kazmeirowicz is a fan favorite and probably Team Captain next year. I don't know. I'm going to have to do media training with some of these young guys to make sure they're all polished up."

"Did you do media training with Evan and David?" I ask.

"No," she says. "They were both naturals on camera. Some people just get it."

"But Evan's always all over social with women and parties and cars," I say. "Surely that can't be good for the brand?"

"I think people feel some of that is part and parcel to an athlete's life," Fiona says. "Though I am sure our fans would be overjoyed to see him settle down. I'd love to fix him up, see him propose to someone. Our own little version of a royal wedding."

"Has the Crush ever had a well-known player get married?"

Fiona thinks about this, her lips pushed to one side. "I don't think so," she says. "Not since the advent of social anyway."

She makes a curious little noise and wanders off without so much as a "see you later." Fiona has not been effusive about my work, which is a bummer. I have the metrics for year-over-year engagement and I know my work is generating lots more traffic than they've ever had on social before. I can't tell if she just doesn't like me, or if maybe she doesn't get what I'm trying to do. I've given her plans, which she approved, but she still doesn't seem to get excited about what I'm doing. She's always sort of professional with a dash of disapproval. I'd kind of hoped for supportive and mentoring. I'd settle for something in between, just a shade warmer than the cold tone I get from her most of the time.

I have been working more video into my feeds, getting Boomerang moments on ice, which have been really popular. I plan to do some pre-game video at the next few games, as well.

Oh well. I sigh and look around the now-empty press room. Guess I'll go back to my hotel room and get my pre-game posts lined up for tomorrow.

Just because I'm a glutton for punishment. And a little bit lonely, to be honest, I shoot Evan a text from the staff bus on the way back to the hotel.

Holly: Good game tonight.

Evan: Thanks. Nice work on social. I'm thumbing through it all now.

Evan: Too much of that rookie's face on display, though. Need to focus on those of us who are most handsome.

Holly: LOL. Noted. I'll get more Chalamet in there tomorrow night. He has good helmet hair.

Evan: His locks are quite luscious.

Holly: Luscious. Good word. Maybe I'll use that in my mullet series.

Evan: You're doing a mullet series?

Holly: Well...a hair series. But there are bound to be a few mullets.

Evan: Hockey hair. It's a tradition.

Holly: I think the mullet tradition is probably about fanned out.

Evan: Never. I'm growing one now.

Holly: That'll attract the ladies.

Evan: You have no idea...

Holly: Speaking of which...Fiona wants to see you settle down.

Evan: Settle down?

Holly: You know. Find a little woman. Put a ring on it.

Evan: Err. Excuse me. I'm having a panic attack.

Evan: Unless the woman she wants me to settle down with is you.

Holly: Definitely not.

Evan: Well then…

Holly: She has royal wedding in her head.

Evan: Am I marrying a princess?

Holly: I suppose that's up to you.

Evan: Have you ever seen the movie Kingsman?

Holly: Yes. Lady with blades for legs. Heads exploding. Cinematic masterpiece.

Evan: You hated it?

Holly: No. I liked it a lot.

Evan: I love you.

Holly: Ummm…

Evan: I mean…your taste in movies.

Evan: Anyway. He says he's always wanted to kiss a princess.

Evan: That's what that made me think of…

Evan: *Crickets* Did I lose you?

Holly: What? No. I was thinking that he does more than kiss the princess.

Evan: Yes. He. Does.

Evan: And all I want to do is teach the princess to skate.

Holly: Well, the princess is not interested.

Evan: I think she is. At least a little.

Holly: I told you, I'm not the girl for you. But we can be friends.

Evan: Ugh. Knife in my heart.

Evan: Dreaded friend-zone.

Holly: Well, I'm not in the market for a boob grab, so...

Evan: I told you, accosted!

Holly: Likely story. Have you ever Googled yourself?

Evan: That sounds dangerous.

Holly: It was for me.

Holly: On that note. Good game. Good luck tomorrow.

Evan: Nighty night, Holly.

When I get into my room, I flop onto the bed with a huge groan. Why does he have to be so fun to talk to? So easy to flirt with? Ugh. I don't want to like the same movies as he does. I don't want to think about all the things we could be doing together. He is a player, pure and simple. He said it himself that marriage makes him have panic attacks. He's not for me. He will only hurt my fragile heart. I can't be thinking about him like this.

But I do. I think about Evan all night long, my fingers starting and deleting new texts over and over again until my eyelids finally get heavy and I fall into a fitful sleep.

TWELVE

EVAN

So of course, after I finished my delightfully flirty text exchange with the lovely Holly Laurent, I did Google myself. I'm not proud of it, as there is a kind unspoken agreement we never do that. You just never really want to know how much is out there and what people are saying. It's like authors or actors who say they never read their own reviews.

And, yeah, I can see why she's shying away. Lots of pictures much like the one I warned her about, only most of them I was glad to participate in, and many of them led to other activities which shall not be named.

She probably thinks I'm a total man-whore and she wouldn't be wrong. And really, what do I want from Holly anyway? I'm not a commitment and royal wedding kind of guy. That's not me, or at least it hasn't been. I'm a one-and-done, no-strings guy. And I can tell it's not who she is at all.

Thing is...I like her. It's not just because she's gorgeous, which she certainly is. It's not just that she's sexy, because she's definitely sensual, as well. It's also because she's good at her job, smart, hard-working. She's funny and doesn't take herself too seriously, but she's also got convictions.

I wonder if she's ever Googled herself? Probably not, right? Since she probably has a perception only moderately famous people have an online presence worth looking at? Okay, maybe that's a stretch.

Well, well, what have we here? Holly has a LinkedIn profile. Nice. It's got a few internships on it, plus a list of extracurricular activities. This job at the Crush is her first real gig, it looks like. Her headshot looks nice and polished.

Of course, that's boring. Next link. This one is a link to her UCLA running profile. She was a distance runner, regional champion in cross-country. Lots of wins next to her name. Color me impressed, and her official Bruins athletic photo is so cute, I find myself wanting to ask her to put on that little white t-shirt and grey running tights just for my own amusement.

Not much else to be found on this girl. She definitely keeps a low profile. It's intriguing, really. I really want to know more about her. I should probably apologize for being a pig. Surely, she thinks very little of me, if she's seen all of these photos all over the web, but when we talk, I feel she really does kind of like me. She says as friends, but is this really the way she sees me? I'm in kind of a grey area here. One, no woman has ever denied me once I've made an offer to get together. She's now done it multiple times. Two, am I more attracted because she keeps saying no? Will my interest fade once I get her into bed, like it always does?

There's only one way to find out, in my estimation.

And either way, I need to apologize and be on my best behavior with her.

Coach tells us the media team is going to be in the hallway doing some video for social media as we head out onto the ice for this game. He says to watch our language and behave for the cameras, as if we're little kids. I, of course, feel like a little kid getting all excited knowing I'll see Holly there. I question if I should go find her before we head out and apologize for acting like a beast.

I should. I'm going to.

I wander out of the locker room and find the woman who gives out media credentials standing with Fiona. The girl is in jeans and a Crush pullover. She looks fourteen and I'd swear she was a fan waiting for an autograph if I hadn't seen her sitting across from Holly's desk the day I went into the office. She gives a little wave as I emerge.

Fiona's bob is sharp and sleek, her suit well-tailored. She narrows her eyes at me as I look around.

"She's not here yet," Fiona says.

"I'm sorry?"

"Holly," she says in a tone that lets me know I'm not going to convince her I'm out here for any other reason. "She's not here yet."

"I wasn't—I was just looking for one of my gloves. Thought I dropped it on my way in from practice."

She raises an eyebrow, not buying it. I shut myself back into the locker rooms, bummed I can't get this off my chest prior to game time.

Georg elbows me as I pull on my skates. "You sick or something?"

"No, why?"

"You're acting bizarre," he says. "You didn't stay out long last night, ditched us the night before. Now you're all quiet."

"Are you my mother now? I'm not sick."

"Well, you're not your usual self," he says. "So, knock it off. Get your head in the game. It's go time."

I let out a laugh and slap him on the back of the head. We get up and huddle, the coach giving us our last words before game time. As we move out into the hallway, Fiona, the girl whose name I don't know, and Holly are all there with their phones. They're asking us to say hi to fans, to call the final score, and to yell out our favorite songs. I push my way to the other side of the hallway so I can end up on Holly's camera, but just as the guy in front of me gets past her, she shuts off her phone and averts her eyes, leaning down and fiddling with her boot. She looks adorable, her long hair in a thick braid, a Crush sweatshirt over skinny jeans tucked into high-heeled boots. I want nothing more than to grab that braid and pull her to me. I want to kiss her.

Fuck. I have to keep going. No time for big displays. And besides, kissing her without her consent, in front of her boss, is not going to win me points.

I keep going, annoyed. We skate out on the ice, the home crowd loudly booing. I keep looking to the edge, where we came from, hoping I can catch her eye as she holds up her phone to get more video. She never looks at me, though, only checks her footage, frowns a little, and heads up to her seat.

We head to the bench and Coach puts Georg and me in as starters. I force myself to focus on the ice, the puck, the guys around me. I drown out the crowd noise and look for openings.

I'm a winger, so I play along the wings, at the outside of the rink. Georg plays interior, always at my side, defending me from defensemen who would try to check me into the glass or snag the puck and send it down to their offensive players.

As one of the New York players comes at me, I maneuver away from the wall, forcing him to skate past me. His skates scrape on the ice as he skids to turn back on me. I pass the puck to Georg, who moves it down closer to the net before dropping back and passing to Chalamet, who skates off with it, close enough to take a shot on goal before getting checked into the glass—but not before he passes the puck back to Georg, who swings it to me as I skate free of my defender, grabbing it and making a short, quick shot past the goalie and into the net.

George skates up and smacks me on the back as we reset. I look around and see Holly, working between her phone and her laptop. She's slipped a pair of glasses on since I last saw her and, damn, it makes her look even more sexy.

I shake my head, trying to get thoughts of her out of my mind so I can play this game. Pointless, even though Georg and I play well together. My mind jumps to Holly again and again. I look over at her, hoping she'll look back, make eye contact. But she never does.

I sit out for the first five minutes of the third period while coach plays the rookie Mikhail on the wing. He's good, scrappy. Not as fast as me but definitely has the look of a killer on the ice. He'll be good in a year or two, definitely has the capability, but the weight of that chip on his shoulder is holding him back.

Coach transitions the whole line on a commercial break. A pop song about being confident comes on and all the women in the arena stand up to sing and dance. Holly grins at this, doing a panoramic sweep of the area with her phone. I watch, totally mesmerized by her smile, until the music fades and the game resumes.

New York's got an enforcer who alternates between playing the wings and the defensive line. He's big and brutal and George absolutely hates him. His name is Viktor Demoskev. Mostly, Georg has kept him out of my line of sight tonight, but I think it's pissing the guy off, because in period three, he's gone berserk, scrapping with Georg and trading verbal barbs that are distinctly not indicative of good sportsmanship.

I'm focused on the net, trying to score my third goal to get us out of a tie with New York. Georg passes the puck and I skate like my life depends on it, only to get crosschecked by the big Russian.

Not gonna lie. I see stars as I fly about two feet to hit the glass, sliding down the wall to hit the ice. It takes me a good minute to realize Georg is right in front of me. His voice sounds muffled. I think he's saying my name. Then the trainers are there, one of them waving a finger in front of me. I look around, confused. I still can't quite hear right.

The trainers pick me up by the armpits and I hear the crowd cheer as we make our way off the ice. As we head into the tunnel. I look up and see her face. Holly's beautiful face. She looks worried.

"Is that AC/DC?" I ask dumbly

Mick, one of our trainers, says, "Yep. *Thunderstruck*. Like you."

This cracks me up for some reason but laughing makes my head hurt. I think I might throw up.

I'M TAKEN TO the New York team's training facility, where they have an in-house sports medicine team on hand. I'm feeling a little less scrambled as they divest me of my uniform and put me into a pair of shorts and a t-shirt.

They take me to the MRI first. Not my first rodeo for concussion protocol, and even I can tell my brains got cooked on that one. My knee is also swollen and hurting—I landed funny when I hit the boards. The team doctors decide to send me home early, too much loud protesting on my end. We've got one more game in this road series.

Mick travels back with me that night, telling me he'll be my roommate for a couple of days until I'm cleared by the doctors. I spend most of the next two days in a dark room, pissed off at the massive headache I have. Mick forces me awake every few hours, making me do light exercises.

By the third day, everyone is home and I'm back in the MRI for another scan. Three wins in the books, no thanks to my sorry ass. I head into the Crush training facility to meet with Scott, the team physician, and Coach Brown.

"Got your noodle cooked, hey boy?" Coach asks.

"Did," I agree, grabbing a chair and popping open a can of soda.

"Feeling' better?" he asks.

"Yeah, today I am," I say. "Not so soggy."

"Good," he says. "Doc, what's the verdict?"

"His scans look better," the doctor says. "His reactions are stronger today. I think he'll be good to go in a couple of days as long as he stays upright. Pull him if you see any lingering symptoms, though."

"You got it," Coach says. He turns to me, "Dodged a bullet, thank God. I need you out there."

Relieved to be cleared, I head back home on strict instructions to rest the next two days and then report back for practice. I'm also, finally, given clearance to look at screens, which was prohibited by my short-term roommate, Mick. I check my phone, hoping to see a text or call from Holly, but there is nothing from her.

Georg, however, has sent me a few video links. The first is the video of the impact I took. I cringe watching it, but I make myself watch it twice more before looking at the second video, or Georg trying to pummel Demoskev during the post-game handshake. A fight breaks out that is quickly pulled apart, with both Georg and Demoskev hurling insults at each other in Russian.

This makes me laugh a little, and I send Georg a text thanking him for sticking up for me.

Evan: Thanks for beating up the bully for me.

Georg: No problem. I hate the fucker.

Evan: Aw. You'll always have Sochi.

Georg: Fuck Sochi. Fuck that guy.

Evan: LOL

Georg: You better?

Evan: Good to go in a few days.

Georg: Need me to send you a stripper-gram?

Evan: Nope.

Georg: Call-girl with a deep throat?

Evan: Definitely not. Germs.

Georg: Saran-wrapped then?

Evan: Stop. Jesus.

Georg: Just trying to help you heal faster.

Evan: I'm good. I just want to wallow in the dark and feel sorry for myself.

Georg: ....

Georg: Okay. Suit yourself. Get better, fuckface.

Shaking my head and grinning like a loon, I check my phone again for any sign of Holly. Fuck it, I'll just call her.

It rings four times before heading to voice mail.

I don't have the heart to leave a message.

And I really do wallow and sulk for the rest of the night.

THIRTEEN

HOLLY

Evan got hammered by that big New York player. Holy cow. I think I actually yelped when it happened, and it took every ounce of self-control to stay in my seat and not go racing down the stairs to get a closer look, to make sure he was okay.

As it was, I could tell he was concussed when they brought him out of the rink and into the tunnel. And I felt sick about it, like maybe it was my fault. I'd ignored him during the few moments before the game. He came to my side of the hallway to get on camera and I'd blown him off, pretended to check my boot just to avoid facing what I knew was going to be some inexplicable chemistry.

He looked for me several times while he was on the ice. I faked being hard at work. Which I was, but not so hard at work that I wasn't able to catch each glance he cast my way. Every single one went straight to my belly. Butterflies isn't a word that covers what I felt when I knew his eyes were on me. More like stampeding horses.

I'm back home, now, prepping for a meeting with Fiona and Bud. My stomach is nervous for a different reason. I'm really worried Fiona isn't pleased with my work. I hope I don't lose my job because I'll be crushed.

I turn on some music as I review all of my posts and plans-in-prep for the meeting. Even though I promised I wouldn't, I review the images and video from Evan's injury for the millionth time. Every time, there's that glance. The one moment when he loses his concentration, looks my way. And BAM, he goes flying. I can't help but feel it's my fault.

Maybe someone else noticed? Maybe I'll be fired for distracting the star player. I would deserve it.

The Black Keys' *Never Gonna Give You Up* plays as I review everything for the meeting, that nervous pit of anxiety growing. It's actually good for calming the nerves a little, but it makes my mind wander back to gorgeous Evan. I should probably call and check on him, right? Apologize for getting him hurt?

When I get to the administrative offices, I find Fiona and Bud in the conference room. Bud smiles brightly as I enter, standing and shaking my hand. Fiona says hello but doesn't get up. Behind me, the rest of the media team trails in to take seats and I find myself relieved. If they're all here, then this isn't just about me or my work.

"Good morning," I say, chipper. "How's everyone doing today?"

"Very good," Bud says. "You?"

"I'm well, thank you," I lie.

Fiona sits forward in her chair once everyone is seated. "So, team," she says. "I've been thinking about our media management tactics lately. According to the analytics reports, a good portion of our social media demographic is female. We've got a strong number of males in the stands and reading traditional news sources, but the fans who follow our social, Foundation work, and other marketing efforts are primarily female."

She makes it sound like she pulled all those numbers on her own. I smile blandly as she talks, trying not to give away my annoyance at the fact she's taking credit for my research. I gave her that information—but okay.

74

"I want to brainstorm on how we can really bump up our engagement with that female demographic. The guys are playing really well, so I'm not worried about filling seats or attracting our male fans. They'll still show up for promo nights and other special events. But I think there is work to be done with women, so let's discuss our options there."

I pipe in then. "I've been working all angles of social. I've got shout-outs going on Snapchat before each game now. I'm thinking of running contests to make it more specific. Like, enter to win and Georg Kolochev can blow you a kiss on Snapchat or whatever."

Someone giggles and says, "He'd probably blow more than a kiss if you let him."

A few other people laugh but Fiona is a rock. She shakes her head. "He has a reputation, but whatever. That's a decent idea. Flesh it out and let me know the plan. What else?"

"I've been doing a hairstyle series on Instagram, playing up on the old idea that all hockey players have mullets. Women seem to be responding well—we have some really handsome players on our team and they are very stylish to boot. It's been fun. And we did a favorite song series, but I think I might do round two focused on their favorite ballads."

"Okay, those are some good prospects," Fiona says. She looks to the rest of the team, and they all throw out ideas for their own areas of engagement. Out of the corner of my eye, I see Kacey King, the blonde reporter who seemed to have a thing for Evan after the first game of the season, wander in and go to Fiona's office.

As the meeting ends, I've got a few new marching orders. I feel out-of-sorts, for some reason, stressed out. I can't figure out why. I sit at my cubicle, but I can't concentrate, so I get up and head to the restroom. As I'm washing my hands, Kacey King comes in. She's in a tight, royal blue dress that really shows off her curvy figure. She looks me up and down, her blue eyes bright and cunning. Her mouth turns up in a smirk, red lips gleaming from a fresh lipstick application.

"I was hoping I'd meet you," she says.

"Me?" I ask, confused.

"Yes, the social media guru. You've really breathed new life into the team's feeds. Nice job."

"Oh, Thanks."

"You know," she says, putting her hands on the sink and leaning into my space, "I heard from my friend Fiona that Evan has taken a bit of an interest in you."

"Oh, I don't know about that...we've only spoken once or twice."

"Must have been quite a conversation, Fiona says he asked for permission to teach you to skate."

A little laugh escapes my lips. "Yes, he did say something about it."

"Look," Kacey says, "I think you know the team has a strict no-fraternization policy. And Evan knows this because he's fucked an employee right out of a job once before. So, don't think this is new territory for him, and don't think that he gives two shits if you lose your job. He's a stud and studs need to rut, if you know what I mean."

"Did he rut with you?" I ask sweetly.

"Oh honey," Kacey says, "I can't be rattled that easily."

"And you think I can?"

"Hmm." She sighs dramatically and stands up straight, turning to focus on herself in the mirror. "Well, I do like what you're doing for the team. I hope you don't end up getting fired for fucking the players."

"Players, plural?"

She smiles and winks. "Stay away from Evan Kazmeirowicz."

I try not to let my jaw hit the floor as she walks out, the threat implicit in her words and tone.

Rattled, I make my way out of the restroom and just keep walking, headed outside into the sun for some rejuvenation. I finally pull out my phone and call Pam.

"Hey honey," she says. "Out on our lunchtime walk?"

CRUSHED

"Yeah," I say," But I also needed to get out of the office. I just had the weirdest run-in with this local television reporter."

"Which one?"

"Kacey King," I say. "You know, the one that did the flirty interview with Evan after the first game?"

"Oh yeah, I remember her. Blonde? Big rack?"

"That one. And a nasty streak," I say. "She basically threatened to tell my boss I'm screwing the players in order to get me fired. Said Evan—and I quote—fucked someone out of her job once before."

"Yikes," Pam says. "Is that true?"

"No clue, but I feel like I would've heard that rumor, though, you know?"

"I'd think so. Sounds like the kind of water cooler thing that one hears, especially when the player in question is sniffing around."

"I'm, like, a thousand percent sure that Kacey and Evan got it on," I say. "No reason to get territorial unless you feel threatened, right?"

"Agreed," Pam says, "that bitch is trying to land her a man."

"Do you think she just has high hopes, or am I right they've already done it?"

"Probably the latter. Holly, his record seems to be love 'em and leave 'em. She probably thinks she can be different. The one who turns his attention away from whoring around."

I cringe. "Ugh. Who knows how many women he's done it with? Why do I like this guy? He probably has chlamydia."

"Genital warts," Pam says.

"Or Gonorrhea."

"Herpes?" she suggests.

"Okay, Okay," I laugh, "I'm sufficiently grossed out now. I think I can go back to work and not be distracted by thoughts of Evan."

"Just think of him with rot-dick and you'll be refocused on work in a jiffy."

"Eew?" I say, giggling. "Thank you and I love you."

We hang up and I go back to work focused once more, completely convinced that Evan Kazmeirowicz is not worth my time and energy. Kacey King can have him.

FOURTEEN

EVAN

I've decided to go the romantic route with Holly. I haven't spoken to her since our text exchange in New York. I'm a little offended she didn't at least check in to make sure I was okay after my injury, though I did see she was posting Get Well messages from fans and giving Twitter updates on my condition. So obviously she's been following my recovery. Which gives me hope.

I decide to sneak in before the office opens for the morning, on my way to the gym. I figure I'll just leave these flowers for her, and let the ball stay in her court. But just as I sneak in the back way, past Bud's office, Fiona Starling comes striding toward me.

Today, she's in a black blouse with a deep V-neck and a knee-length pencil skirt. She has on very high heels to accentuate her long legs. Fiona is an attractive woman, older than me but certainly very put-together. She's always been a little cold for my taste. I don't know her well because she just doesn't strike me as all that interesting. I envision her as a bit of a cold fish in bed.

Today, though, she gives me a cat's smile, all full of mischief. I'm immediately taken aback.

"Up early today, are we?" she asks. "Must be feeling better?"

"Yep. Back at the gym for the first time in a week. Looking forward to it. Feeling pent up."

She looks me up and down. The expression on her face is hungry and it weirds me out.

"Pent up, huh?" she asks. "That's a terrible feeling."

"Uh-huh," I answer, confused. What the hell is happening right now?

"Who are the flowers for?" she asks.

"For a friend who deserves them."

"Well, this friend must be very special indeed, to get your attention," Fiona says.

I bite the inside of my lip. "Look, Fiona, I know you're a stickler on the no-fraternization policy. I assure you nothing is happening with me and my friend. She's been a total pro."

"Your friend, meaning Holly," she says flatly. She looks like she swallowed a lemon.

"Holly," I confirm. "She's not interested in me. We're just friends."

She steps closer to me, so now we're nearly chest-to-chest. She's a tall woman, I just realized.

"I'd love to visit with you sometime," she says, her voice lower than usual. "Privately. To discuss that fraternization policy."

A quick drop of the eyes confirms her nipples are rock hard beneath that thin top. Oh shit. The married and seemingly uptight Fiona Starling is coming onto me. *WTF?*

I step back just slightly. "Well, I'm not sure what there is to discuss," I say. "I'm certain you've got good reasoning for it. And I'm sure it applies to all employees, even management."

She squares her shoulders and looks over her shoulder, as if she's worried someone has seen this little exchange. Then she gives a nod and says, "Well, I will hope to see you soon. I'd love to pick your brain since you're clearly interested in what the media team is doing here."

"Yeah, sure, I'm always happy to help promote the team."

She looks around again and says something about needing to prep for a meeting. I say goodbye and she walks away, leaving me flummoxed in the hallway, wondering when the hell Fiona decided she wanted to come onto me. That's new. And strange. I think I need a wash off now.

Shake it off. Leave the flowers for Holly. Get on with the day.

Of course, my plan to drop the flowers and run is thwarted again because overachiever Holly is already at her cubicle when I come around the corner. She looks up as I approach, and she can't hide the smile spreading across her face. Goddamn. It's like the sun came out. A beautiful thing just got more beautiful.

"Good morning, Miss Laurent." I hold out the flowers. "These are for you. My apology for being a loser."

"You're not a loser," she says, taking the proffered flowers and setting them on her desk. "You're a winner. Welcome back. How are you feeling?"

"Much better, thank you. Slightly strained tendon in my knee. Concussion in the old noggin. All cleared for play, though."

"That was a brutal hit you took," she says, frowning. It's cute. Why is every face she makes so cute? "I felt a little sick watching it."

"It was a bloody dirty move, is what it was," I say.

"Georg thought so too. He defended your honor afterward."

I grin. "I know. I saw the footage."

"Kazochev is hotter than ever," she says. "People ship you two even more after that."

"Well, he's not my type," I say. "Too hairy."

She laughs out loud. "I don't think I believe you have a type, Evan, I believe your type is all."

"Oh," I say, putting my hand to my chest. "You wound me. I do want to apologize for that picture again. I really wasn't out to meet anyone. She asked for a selfie and put my hand there."

Holly looks skeptical. "Whatever, no need to apologize. You don't answer to me, Evan."

"But I need you to know," I insist, "I get waylaid like this all the time. Women think they own me, think I'll screw anything that moves. And when I was younger, maybe I was partial to it."

"When you were younger, like last year?" she asks with a smirk. "Look, your sex life is your business. It's not for me to judge."

"Well," I say, leaning closer. "I wish it was."

Her eyes go wide.

"Look, Holly, I'd love a chance with you. To get to know you. I don't just want—I mean, I want to, but not *just* that. Am I making any sense? I feel like a stammering teenager."

I wipe my forehead and make an exaggerated face. She giggles.

"You make me nervous and it's very unusual, because I rarely get nervous," I admit.

"Well, I guess I kind of feel the same," she says, suddenly blushing and acting shy. She looks at her shoes. She's fucking gorgeous.

"Will you think about it?" I ask. "We have a day off in Anaheim. Maybe we could go sight-seeing? Purely platonic. Unless…it isn't."

"I'll think about it," she says. She tilts her head. "Can I change the subject for a second?"

"Sure."

"I keep hearing about All-Star voting," she says. "Is that a goal of yours? To get voted onto the All-Star Team?

I nod. "It is. Georg too. And I want team votes for Captain once Chalamet retires."

"Cool," she says. "I'm working on some new contests and polls. I can throw in some promotion for fans to vote on All-Stars. I'll probably have to promote our top scorers. Not sure if Fiona will let me focus on just you."

"Oh, she might," I say. I don't want to out Fiona for her odd little innuendo-infused hallway meeting this morning, but I feel fairly certain about her being okay with promoting me anywhere, anytime.

"She's weird about stuff," Holly says. "I'll run it past her, though."

My phone buzzes in my pocket, then. I pull it out and take a look. It's a text from Kacey King. "Sorry," I say. "Give me a second?"

Holly nods. "I need to get to work anyway, no worries."

I look down and roll my eyes at the very first line.

Kacey: Hey, stud. Welcome back to the game, I hear. Can we get thirty minutes for an exclusive on your return to the ice after the hit you took in New Jersey?

Evan: Talk to Fiona to set it up.

Kacey: Did. Approved. When is good?

Evan: We're home tomorrow and then we leave for California.

Kacey: Tomorrow then? Before you suit up?

Evan: I don't know. Let me see how I feel.

Kacey: I can help you prep, if you'd like.

Evan: Nah. I'm all good. Just saying, I haven't worked out in days. Might need time to warm up.

Kacey: I can help you warm up, too.

Evan: Keep it professional, K

Kacey: Not what you said when you had your head between my legs.

Evan: Last warning or no interview.

Kacey: Killjoy. Okay. Text me tomorrow with a time.

I look up and see Holly is back at her desk, studying some kind of analytics on her laptop. I take the few steps and look over her shoulder, putting my hands on the back of her chair. Even from here, I can smell her shampoo. It smells like mint. She smells like food, oh my god. Not perfume or flowers or some shit. She smells good enough to eat. Sweet and fresh. I suppress a groan. My cock even twitches in my pants, which is horrifyingly teenager of me. What is it about this woman who makes me so crazy like this?

"What's all this?" I ask, very close to her ear.

She jumps and lets out a little yelp. I laugh out loud. "Sorry, darlin'," I say. "I didn't think you were actually engrossed in all that mumbo jumbo. I thought you were just pretending to ignore me."

She turns and looks at me, her cute nose all wrinkled. "Contrary to popular belief, I do not sit around thinking about Evan Kazmeirowicz all day long. I do actually have a job to do."

"And you're quite good at it," I say, leaning in. I whisper, "But I think you're lying about the first part, because I sure as hell think about you all day."

There is great satisfaction in watching the subtle ways a woman shows she is aroused. The slight intake of breath. The flush on her cheeks, and lower. The outline of hard nipples appearing beneath her shirt. The way she squeezes her legs together.

"Anaheim?" I ask again, softly so only she can hear it.

She swallows and nods.

After a quick look around to make sure no one was around to catch me, I lean in and give her a quick peck on the cheek. "You won't regret it," I say, every word a promise.

I'm out of there before I can get accosted by Fiona again, and on a call to Scott to ask if I can get out of this interview with Kacey.

"Fiona clear it?" he asks. I can hear the whir of a machine in the background.

"Are you walking on a treadmill?"

"Got a treadmill desk," he says. "I was getting too fat sitting on my ass all day."

"You run more than anyone I know," I say. "I find it hard to believe you sit more than ten minutes a day."

"Whatever. Take the interview. Fiona's the boss on media matters, and people are curious if you'll be in prime shape for this run of games. I mean, shit, you only missed two games and you got your clock cleaned. You actually sure you're good to go, man?"

"I'm good," I say. I listened to doc's orders for seven days. I've worked out, been on the ice. I feel good. No worries."

"Okay, well, let me call Kacey and set up the interview. We'll make sure it's short, sweet, and gets you focused on the ice in no time."

I groan in response.

"What's wrong with you?" he asks. "You've never had an issue with media before."

"Kacey's just…" I groan again.

"She wants to fuck you. Again. Big deal. Just do what you gotta do," he says.

"I feel personally victimized by that statement. Are you suggesting I let her have her way with me?"

"Whatever," he says. "She gives you good press. Good press means All-Star votes. Think of it that way."

"I won't fuck her," I say, "but I'll do the interview."

"Of course you will," he says. "I'll set it up. Call you back with the details."

I shake my head and hang up. Fine. I'll do the stupid interview. But only because I know I've got a date with Holly on the horizon.

FIFTEEN

HOLLY

Evan is holding my hand as I fumble my way around the rink. I feel like a baby, learning to walk for the first time. Or a zombie, all stiff-legged and totally lacking coordination.

"I'm so bad at this," I complain with a laugh. "I thought we were going sight-seeing?"

"I just had this vision of teaching you to skate," he says. "Hang in there. It gets easier."

"I don't know about that." I look down at the skates. "I'm used to my running shoes."

"Do you still run?" he asks as he moves behind me, his hands at my waist to hold me steady. "Try not to lock your knees. Just let yourself move like you normally would."

"I do, yes. Every day almost. It really helps me decompress."

"Did you start running for any specific reason?"

"Um, I guess I just realized it helped me tune out stress," I say, trying to will my body to relax. "My parents had already divorced by the time I was in high school. My mom and her new husband moved to France like the minute I started college. My dad's job had always taken him overseas, and he

86

eventually made his home in Saudi Arabia. So, it's safe to say I've mostly been on my own to figure things out."

"They fought a lot? And you ran to shut it out?"

"Yeah. Started running in middle school, actually. Got good at it. I was determined not to allow myself to be a pawn in my parent's legal battle over money, so I pushed myself through high school, got the attention of the UCLA cross country coaches."

Talking like this has helped me relax, and I feel myself getting more comfortable on the skates. Evan moves back to my side, taking my hand again as we keep making our way around the ice.

"Well, you must have been damn good, then. Maybe we can go for a run together sometime. I must confess seeing you all sweaty and in some tight running shorts is kind of a fantasy of mine," he says with a wicked smirk on his too-handsome face.

I roll my eyes and slip a little, my concentration utterly broken. Evan is there in a heartbeat, pulling me close to his body, his arm snaking around my waist. We're not moving, and I'm wrapped in his arms. He looks down at me and before I can say a word or make a joke, his lips are on mine.

At first, I stiffen. Do I want to go there with him?

The answer is: I do. I want him. I reach up and run my fingers through his hair, finding it as silky as it has been in my dreams. I move my hands to his face, his thick, short beard covering a chiseled face.

I let out a little moan and he uses it as an opening to deepen the kiss, his tongue finding mine. We kiss and kiss until I'm breathless. When I pull away, I feel my cheeks heat with a blush that I'm sure has spread to other parts of my now-overheated body.

"I knew it would be good." He takes my hand and helps me get started skating again.

"You did, did you?" I ask, grinning, still blushing. "What if I'd had tuna breath or something?"

"I like tuna okay," he says, grinning back, "and your cheeks are all pink now. It's lovely on you."

There's been music playing the whole time, mostly classic rock songs. "You like classic rock?" It's my feeble attempt at distracting myself from the way he just said "lovely" in his sexy accent.

"I do," he says. "Hockey tradition. Like the mullet. It grows on you."

"I like it okay, but I like modern music better. Pop-punk, alt rock. Fall Out Boy, The Black Keys, Twenty-One Pilots."

He nods. "I know the first two, not the last one."

"They're a little different," I say. "Really, I like most music. I have different favorites for different paces."

The Police's *Every Breath You Take* comes on and I smile at him. "I love this song."

"Me too," he says. "I love the Police and I love Sting. Did you know he and his wife are like yoga gurus?"

"I didn't," I say, laughing. "Do you do yoga?"

"Hell no. I'm bloody well sure I'd pull a muscle or something. Not flexible enough."

"I like yoga. It's very relaxing."

He grunts his dissent. "Sorry about your parents," he says. "You don't talk to them much?"

"Every couple of months. I mean, they love me, and they check in, but they were both so unhappy for so long, it just felt like they both needed a total restart. I'm a big girl. It's no big deal."

"My parents are also divorced. My father is from the Ukraine, my mother is from Boston. She was the one who insisted I go to an English school."

"Is that where you learned to play hockey?"

"I've been on skates since I could stand upright, I think," he says. "I certainly started skating before I went to school. But they had a competitive team, and I was a competitive kid."

"Sounds like a good fit, but when did you realize you could make it as a professional player?"

He shrugs. "Always? Is that cocky?"

I laugh. "A little."

He stops us and pulls me close again, his lips brushing mine. This time, the kissing becomes more intense, deeper, and I feel like I'm being pulled into an undertow that I might not be able to escape. I can't seem to help myself either. I turn to putty when his lips are on mine.

When he pulls away, I feel a little dazed. He looks so gorgeous. I've never seen a man that looks like him, who makes me feel the way he makes me feel. Of course, I'm not going to tell him this. He already has a huge head.

"So, what do you think?" he asks.

"About?"

"Skating, of course."

"Oh," I say. "It's pretty fun, I guess. It would be hard to do it in thick pads and with a stick and having to track a puck, though."

"We'll get there."

"Oh, we? No," I say. "I don't think I need to actually play hockey to promote it."

"I disagree," he says. "Tell me about the blue line."

I laugh but see he really is trying to quiz me. So I answer that, plus a few more questions about the game and the basic rules. He corrects me a couple of times, but the best part are the kisses I get between each question.

We make our way off the ice, to the benches where we pull off our skates. Evan goes to take the skates back to wherever he got them from. His phone buzzes on the bench. I glance at it and see it's from Kacey King.

Kacey: Thanks for the other night...you were awesome.

Evan returns, all smiles until he sees my face. It must be drained of color, because I suddenly feel totally cold and empty. And a little bit sick. I point to his phone where it sits face up on the bench, right where he left it. "Kacey says you were awesome the other night." I know my tone is bitchy, but I don't care.

He gives me a grin, but it falters a bit. "Yeah, I did an interview with her before the home game. No biggie."

"It's a biggie to me." All of my good feelings have been sucked away, like a balloon deflating as it circles its way to the ground. "Evan, I—"

"You what? You expect I'd just sleep around with anyone and everyone?"

"I had a fiancé who cheated on me. I haven't been with anyone since, because obviously"—I point a thumb at myself—"trust issues. And I keep telling myself that I should walk away from a guy like you."

"What kind of guy am I?"

"One who, you know, sleeps with lots of women. Who can't be tied down."

His lips press together. I can see him trying to figure out how to respond. "Holly, I'm not going to pretend I don't have a history. But I'm not interested in Kacey. And I haven't slept with anyone in months. I'm interested in you, and not just for sex."

"I just...she confronted me the other day at work." I feel tears welling up in my eyes. "She threatened to make me lose my job if I didn't stay away from you. And I can see she's really trying to get your attention."

"She can't make you lose your job, Holly."

"She can. She knows Fiona," I insist. "She wants you, and she won't stop until she gets you."

"Don't I get a say? I told you I don't want Kacey." I can hear the irritation in his tone. I've made him mad. Everything good that happened between us today is now ruined.

Suddenly I feel trapped, in almost a claustrophobic way. I need get away from him and away from the helpless intoxication I feel whenever I'm with him. "I'm gonna go, Evan,

I'm sorry." I say, grabbing my shoes and sprinting towards the exit. Running *is* my talent after all.

I slip into the ladies' lounge at the front of the building and plop down onto a soft bench, so I can put my shoes back on. I request an Uber and wait it out inside the lounge until the driver alerts me he is arriving. Only then do I hit the front exit. I manage to hold onto my pathetic tears until my butt is safely planted in the back seat of my ride.

Just barely, and not for long, though.

Because as we drive away, Evan comes striding outside, his face a mask of concern. Still handsome as hell, but I can tell he is thoroughly offended by my behavior. Facing him at work now is really going to suck.

I go straight to Pam's apartment, desperately in need of my friend's shoulder to cry on.

And one huge-ass reality check.

SIXTEEN

EVAN

Anaheim. Game five of our as-yet-undefeated season. I should be pumped. I should be listening to some classic rock, thinking only about how I'm going to skate today, and how many goals I'm going to score.

Instead, I'm sitting on the bench in the locker room, half-dressed, looking at pictures and videos I took of Holly while we were skating. I took one in slow motion, a short one as she took her first, gliding movements on her own. It's from the back, her gorgeous hair hanging long, her arms out wide. As she turns, laughing, the video goes blurry.

I do have my own social media. I have a Facebook page meant to allow fans to connect with me, though I never check it. I have Instagram, too, but I only login every few months, and usually only to repost stuff from the team. And I have Twitter. Twitter, where all boob-grab pictures go to cause me distress and fuck up my relationsh—

Whoa. Did I just *ship* myself with Holly?

I think I did. Scratch that, I totally fucking did.

Georg flops down next to me and says, "What are you over here moping about?"

"Not moping."

"Sure looks like it," he says in a judgey voice. "Do you know I was just balls-deep in a puck bunny ten minutes ago? In a supply closet full of mops and buckets and shit."

"Sounds romantic." My sarcasm can't be helped.

"Since when do you care about romance?"

"Fair enough," I say with a shrug, because he's right. Romance has never been my forte.

On a whim, I decide to post the video of Holly on my Instagram page. I caption it 'Skate Training. New Recruit.' before closing out my account and tossing my phone into the locker so I can finish getting dressed.

Someone's got the Rolling Stones playing from a Bluetooth speaker. Normally, this would be just up my alley and I'd be asking them to blast it. But the song *Beast of Burden* comes on, and it just depresses me.

Holly totally ghosted after seeing the text from Kacey. I suppose I understand. The text was totally meant to suggest we'd done something more than just an interview. I'm not even sure it was just Kacey's text that bothered Holly. I think it was more…me. I think she's seen all the junk pointing to the "douchebag womanizer" sign above my head, and she panicked.

Whatever. I've got a game to play. I'll figure out how to get Holly back in my orbit after we win this game.

We head out through the tunnel, the media team back in place, having us make funny faces at the camera for Snapchat. Holly nods as I pass, and I blow her a kiss. She blushes and moves to the guy behind me.

Anaheim has this long-ass intro video with a light show and a recap of the previous game. I swear it's like ten minutes long and only when it ends do they let us out on the ice. Of course, we get booed because it's what's expected for visitors on road games. Then the lights go down again, and they introduce their starters and play *Enter Sandman* by Metallica.

They've actually got a player called The Sandman. He played for Nashville for a couple of years before getting traded to Anaheim. He's known for crosschecks that actually knocked dudes out. Lights out. Talk about a hard hit. I have been instructed to stay as far away from him as possible. Interesting how the team is playing into this guy's reputation by using this as their intro song.

I'm not starting tonight, which is annoying, so I sit on the bench spinning my stick around, legs bouncing with nervous energy, while the game gets started. Chalamet is out on the ice in my place, Georg at his left.

I look around and find Holly staring at me. She looks at her phone, then back at me with wide eyes. She must have seen the video I posted. She points to her screen and I give a quick nod and then look away. If I focus on her, I'll just end up taking a dump like I did in the last game.

Coach puts me in on a line change, when The Sandman heads back to the bench. A Justin Bieber song plays while we skate out, which is a weird choice. It's also weird I know it's Justin Bieber, I guess.

Anaheim is out for blood tonight. The crowd here is rowdy, loud, and ready to see some fighting. Check after check pushes my teammates to the limit, particularly young Mikhail, who ends up taking a wild swing at an Anaheim player after he gets pushed into the glass for the fourth time.

I feel good, though. The energy just pushes me to work harder. Play harder. I score one in the first period, one in the second period. In the third, they tie it up with two goals right in a row. It makes the crowd go even crazier. Coach has his best line on forward, with me and Chalamet on the wings, Georg at center.

We strike forward, fast and furious, moving the puck down the ice, only for Chalamet to get checked. The resulting call puts us on a Power Play with only two minutes left on the clock. The noise in the arena is deafening, Anaheim pushing back against us, fighting for control of the puck.

Chalamet takes a shot on goal that pings off the top of the net. We hang back and wait for Anaheim to bring it back to us, and Georg, game face fierce, goes right after it. He makes a run with it, shooting it straight at the goalie, who falls on top of it.

We just keep pressing and as the clock dwindles, Georg finds an opening to get to me, just as The Sandman swings my way. I fake right, toward the glass, and he falls for it, giving me just the opening I need to get a shot off.

It's like slow motion, watching the puck sail up and over the goalie's helmet, into the back of the net. The buzzer goes off just seconds later. Georg is there, jumping on my back, crazy yelling about "fucking ducks," as we skate back, high on adrenaline, to line up.

We head back to shower and change, the locker room electric. Five wins in a row is not a bad way to start a season. I sit on the bench as Coach and one of the trainers looks me over for any sign that the game may have aggravated my concussion.

With the all clear, Coach rubs the top of my head and says, "If I wasn't so damn old, I'd name my firstborn after you, young man. You are on fire this season. Keep it up."

Mikhail, on the other hand, hasn't fared as well. He sulks across from me, rubbing his wrist.

"You okay, kid?" I ask, lifting my chin and eyeballing his rapidly-swelling joint.

"Fucking Sandman," he growls. "I want to punch his teeth in."

"Seems to be the sentiment about the guy. He wants you in a coma, though, so that fight doesn't seem fair." I nod at his wrist. "You get that checked out yet?"

"It's fine," he says, but he's still rubbing at it.

"Swollen," I say. "At least have them take a look, give you some ice."

He stares blades at me for a minute before getting up and stalking away.

"Nice talking to you, too," I say lightly as I grab my phone.

There are texts from Holly.

Holly: Evan. Video of me? Really?

Holly: 400,000 likes before end of game.

Holly: Ever heard of keeping a low profile?

Holly: People want to kill me now. It literally says, "I want to kill that bitch, whoever she is."

Holly: Good game. Hat trick. Woohoo!

I grin and check my post. It does, indeed, have more than 400,000 likes and about a hundred comments, including the one she mentioned, though most are like, "Aw, cute." I block the one jerky person and delete her comment, then text Holly back.

Evan: I blocked the one weirdo. Most thought it was cute. Can't see your face.

Holly: Still. Anyone who works with me will know it's me.

Holly: I'll probably lose my job now.

Evan: You won't. There's nothing inappropriate about it. Just teaching you to skate.

Holly: Ugh.

Evan: I'm sorry. I just thought it was sweet.

Holly: I don't want people thinking I'm one of your...what do you call them?

Evan: Puck bunnies.

Holly: Barf. Yes. That.

Evan: They won't.

Holly: They will. And you know it.

Evan: I'll take it down if it's that big a deal.

Holly: No. Too late now.

I'm not sure what else to say, so I just put my phone down and head to the showers. Most of the guys are out now, so I take my time then head back to get dressed. Georg asks if I want to go out for a beer and I agree. Why sit around feeling crappy anyway? We just won. I just killed it on the ice. I should not be sitting around worried about whether or not some woman I'm not even dating is worried about a social media post which didn't even identify her.

In the cab on the way to the bar, Georg elbows me in the ribs. "When did you become such a brooding bastard?"

"I'm not," I say. "I'm going out. All good here."

"I feel like I don't even know you anymore," he says, mock crying.

I roll my eyes at him and laugh. "I'm the same me."

"Liar," he says, pulling a flask out of his jacket pocket. He takes a swig and offers it to me. I hold up my hands and shake my head. "At least, please, please, pick up a chick tonight. I'm concerned for your libido."

I laugh again. "You're stupid. And single-minded. Seriously."

"That Kacey is still gunning for you, bro. I saw the piece before our home game. She looooves you," he singsongs in my ear making me want to punch him.

"I told you, not going back for seconds. She tried. Offered. I said no."

"Why?" he asks.

"Because I don't like her very much. She's not a very nice person."

"Since when do you give a fuck?"

"Since now," I say. "I'm ready to find someone nice, maybe make a thing of it."

Georg looks like I really did punch him in the mouth rather than just think about it. "Huh? Does this have to do with the girl you took skating? Oh yeah, I saw your video, lover boy. Are you hiding this girl from me?"

My phone buzzes.

Scott: Congrats on tonight. You are earning those bonuses. Money city.

Evan: Thanks. Felt good out there.

Scott: No head issues?

Evan: Nope. All clear. Good.

Scott: Awesome. Have a good night.

Georg thankfully doesn't press me any more about Holly. We find a small bar where he drinks a few too many and I drink enough to take the edge off. We talk about how much he hates Viktor Demoskev, how he hopes we can play All-Star together.

We don't stay out late, returning to the team hotel, finding the bar there hopping with women and other players. I see no sign of Holly, but Fiona is there. She gives me bedroom eyes, which is a surefire way to get me to head in the other direction right about now. I just avoid the whole scene, handing wasted Georg off to one of our third line defensemen before heading up to the room.

I don't know when things changed for me, but I realize I meant it when I told Georg I was tired of the whole game with women and alcohol and whatever. Maybe it's that I'm nearing thirty, or that I've got renewed career goals to work on. Maybe it's the mystery of Holly Laurent, because she really is still a mystery.

I turn on a movie, falling asleep with thoughts of a brunette beauty still lurking in the back of my mind.

SEVENTEEN

HOLLY

Thank God I didn't have to stay in the hotel with the team last night. I left the game and went straight to Pam's apartment, where we drowned our sorrows in Ben & Jerry's.

Today we're tooling around town, doing a little shopping.

"No, not that store," Pam says as I try to head into a cute little boutique. "They only sell to skinny bitches. This girl is thick." She pats her own rear end.

"Please, spare me the lies. You are in no way thick, but I hear you."

We wander down the sidewalk, mostly window shopping but occasionally dipping in to try things on. Pam tells me that the guy she met at work turned out to be already-married.

"What?" I ask.

"Yep," she says, pulling her mass of blonde hair up on top of her head into a bun as we try on sunglasses. "We'd been making out during late-night rotations at the clinic and one night, this woman comes in and gets in my face. She tells me she saw a picture of us on her husband's phone. Just a normal picture of us together with his arm around me. But still the fucker is married. No Bueno."

"Indeed," I agree. What did you say?"

"Just that I had no idea he was married, and I was sorry. What could I do in that situation? She had the right to be angry."

"Wow," I say with a big sigh. "That's cray."

"And how about you and hockey boy? He posted a video of you?"

I nod and make a face. "Probably get me fired."

"Why? Can't tell it's you."

"I feel like my coworkers will know it's me," I say. "Plus, as you know, I left that whole scene in tears and freaking out like a big weirdo."

"Well obviously he didn't take it personally. I feel like he posted it to prove he really likes you, Holls."

"How could he really like me? He knows, like, nothing about me."

Pam levels me with a look that tells me she thinks I'm being a dummy. "Girl, you ever heard of a thing called chemistry?"

"I mean, yeah," I say as we move on to look at a rack of dresses. "There's chemistry, for sure. When he kissed me, I felt it all the way to my toes, but that's not the same as really knowing someone."

"Well, you've got to start somewhere," Pam says. "And sometimes love just hits you like a ton of bricks, when you're least expecting it."

"Ugh," I say. "And sometimes it hits you like a ton of bricks and leaves you lying half-dead in a ditch. Believe me, Evan Kazmeirowicz is not in love with me, I'm not in love with him, and even if I was, I wouldn't touch it with a ten-foot pole because he's not the kind of guy who falls in love and settles in for life."

Just then, the song *Crazy in Love* comes on in the store. Pam starts dancing and pointing at me. She sings, "My girl Holly's so crazy in love. My girl Holly's so crazy right now."

I wave her off and walk away, hiding my resulting grin. She's silly and loud and brash and I love her. But do I love Evan Kazmeirowicz? No. Definitely not. I lust him—I can admit that much, but love is a whole other ball of wax and he has not earned even my basic trust, so love is impossible.

"I've got some pre-game prep work to do," I say, grabbing her arm and dragging her from the store. Drive us back to your place, Jeeves."

"Only if you promise we can call your hot uncle Troy on the way home," she says. "I miss that silver fox."

"Eww."

"Facetime!" she yells. "I want to see that sexy man's face, or you can walk home!"

I laugh out loud and shush her as we make our way to the car. "You going to come to the game tonight?" I ask, just to change the subject.

She doesn't fall for it. "I said we're calling uncle Troy, girlfriend. So, get on that phone and dial."

I shake my head and Facetime my uncle.

"Hey Holly-dolly," he says, his voice tinny through the speaker phone. "What's up?"

"Hanging with Pam, she says hi."

"Hiiii!" Pam sings, smiling and leaning into the picture for a second.

"Hey Pam, how's my second-favorite girl?"

"Second favorite?" she asks with mock despair.

"You know Holly-dolly is my best girl."

Pam pretends to pout, making us both laugh. Troy says, "Hey, I know you usually sit in the stands to get your social media shots and whatnot, but the LA owners offered me a couple of seats in the suite upstairs for tonight's game. I can't make it because I'm in Vancouver doing some scouting. You and Pam want to sit up there tonight?"

"Heck yes!" Pam yelps.

"I guess that's a yes," I tell him.

"Awesome. Good networking up there. They already know you're killing it for the Crush on social. They'll probably try to steal you away."

"Good," Pam says quietly. "Go work for another team so you can bone that hot guy."

"What did Pam just say?" Troy asks. "I couldn't hear her."

"She said thank you for the seats." I give Pam a pointed look. "She's driving."

"Oh, no problem. And I hate to cut this short, but I've got a practice to watch."

"Okay, love you."

"Love you too," he says.

"Love you!" Pam yells.

"Okay," Troy says with a laugh. "Have fun tonight, girls."

We hang up and head back to Pam's place. We've both picked up cute dresses and decide to dress up for the game since we'll be up in the LA owner's box. As we get dressed, I continue to work on social media, sending out tweets and posting pre-game messaging. I'm not doing the Snapchat messages tonight, because we've launched a "Who's Your Crush?" contest. We'll pick ten winners to get a personal Snapchat shout-out before the home opener for the season. Fiona is beside herself over this idea, loving that we're specifically reaching out to female fans. Of course, we have a few men in the contest, too, which makes it fun. It's the first thing I've done, though, that she's been really excited about, so I guess it's a good thing.

Pam looks ultra-hot in the emerald-green dress she picked out. She's paired it with peep-toe booties and has her hair loose and wild around her shoulders. She's a bit curvier than me, bigger boobs and hips. And she totally owns it. Every pair of eyes will be on her tonight. Next to her, I look plain in my little black dress and knee-high, high-heeled boots. My figure is more athletic than hers. I have much smaller breasts and slim hips. I'm not womanly like her, and while I don't spend a lot of time critiquing myself or comparing myself to others, sometimes I wish I was built like her—a real knockout.

She notices I'm quiet in the car. "You're not going to be all emo tonight, are you?"

"No, of course not."

"Good, because I'm ready to flirt with some hot hockey players."

"Well, it will more be hockey owners and sponsors up in the box. We won't see much of the players unless we happen to run into them after the game," I remind her.

"Then let's happen to run into them after the game," she says with a wink.

EIGHTEEN

EVAN

Georg pulls on his pads and says, "Who's the girl?"

"Well, if you ever actually listened to me when I talk, you might be able to figure it out," I say as I pull my jersey over my head.

He ponders this for a moment. I can see that he's trying to remember our conversations, trying to piece together anything I might have said about a woman.

"Jesus, Georg, don't blow a fuse over it. You need to dry out and maybe your brain will retain information longer."

"I resemble that remark," he says, grinning.

I just roll my eyes. "You want to make All-Star, you probably need your liver functioning."

"My liver functions fine. And more importantly, my legs and arms work well enough to cover your ass on the ice and keep you scoring. And my cock works fine, too, so I can celebrate inside a warm, wet pussy after each win. So, fuck drying out."

I cringe. This is how every conversation about Georg's drinking goes. I try to be funny about it, and then he tries to be funny back. Then I get a little more serious and he gets pissed. It's never caused an issue with our friendship, but I'm guessing someday it might.

CRUSHED

After we're dressed, we huddle up. Our owner, Max, is here for this game and he gives us a pep talk, telling us all how great we're playing and "how damn proud" he is of all of us. He also announces it's time for players to vote on a co-captain for Chalamet. He pats Chalamet on the back as he talks about what an amazing player he's been, about his leadership skills, and about how much the league will miss him. Max makes jokes about Chalamet being the youngest retiree in the nursing home and tells us all how much he wants to see him take home the cup in his last year of play.

We're all asked to cast a vote before we head out. I vote for myself, and then grin, wondering what would happen if everyone did the same.

"What are you grinning about?" Fiona asks as she sidles up to me in the tunnel.

Max walks up beside her and says, "I was wondering the same thing."

"Oh, nothing, just thinking. Hey, on another note, I did the exclusive with Kacey you asked for."

Fiona looks perplexed. "I didn't ask for an exclusive."

"Oh, maybe she asked for it and you approved it?" I ask. "She said she spoke to you about an exclusive before I played the last home game. She wanted to talk about my injury, and if I was going to be able to play out the season."

"I wasn't aware you'd done that," she says. "We are always present for official interviews."

I think my jaw might break from clenching it so hard. "So, you're telling me Kacey King did not, in fact, get approval from you for the interview? She lied?"

Fiona purses her lips and looks pointedly at Max. "Well, I'm sure it was just a miscommunication. We've got so many things going on lately, the request probably just slipped through the cracks. Did it go okay?"

"It was fine." I decide not to mention I'm pretty sure the only reason for the interview was to get me alone.

"Well, no harm done, then," she says quickly as if relieved to find an out from this conversation. "Feel free to call me, though, if you're ever unsure of something. I'm here to support you."

Yeah, I'll bet. She's just one more woman trying to crawl into my bed. To think, not so long ago I might have taken her up on it. Now, I'm just annoyed at the attention and innuendo.

We head out to start the game and as we warm up on the ice, I look around for Holly, realizing she wasn't in the tunnel doing her usual social media work. She's not anywhere in the lower stands. As I try to be inconspicuous with my searching, Georg sidles up next to me and says, "Dude, you see the women in the owner's box tonight? There's a blondie up there I would probably propose to just to get her underneath me in bed."

I look at the box, which is situated between the lower and upper bowl of the arena. Sure enough, there are two women standing at the front. One is curvy, blonde, and laughing wildly at something the man on her left is saying. The other is staring at me. It's Holly. She raises a hand and gives a subtle wave. She looks amazing in a black dress, her hair in a long braid that hangs around her shoulder. I wish I could get a closer look. I wish I could touch the exposed part of her skin. I wish I could kiss her. But I can't, so I just nod to let her know I've seen her.

When the game starts, my head is totally in it. My team just voted for co-captain and I need to show them I can stay on task, even though I know Holly is up in the owner's box with guys probably pawing all over her. Knowing this somehow makes me feel more aggressive and I use it to my advantage.

On the first period break, Georg says, "You know those women?"

"You know one of them," I answer. "Holly, the social media manager for the team. She was in the black."

"Oh? Well, I barely noticed her because of the blonde."

"Maybe a friend of hers," I answer with a shrug. "Don't know."

"Well, I need to meet her."

"Stay in the game, please. Don't think about women. Think about winning this game."

"Aye-aye, captain," he says with a salute.

We skate back out and though Georg gives a long look at the two women, he does seem very focused in the second period, helping me avoid a big collision on the glass, which allows me a chance to wiggle free and take the puck down and into the net for our first score of the game.

I look up and find Holly going wild, jumping up and down and high-fiving her friend. I find myself grinning like an idiot, knowing she's watching. I actually see Max come down and stand with her. They chat for a minute and she pulls something up on her phone. He smiles and pats her on the back amiably. He must have just figured out she's the one who's been killing it on our social media feeds.

Georg is relentless in the second break. "Dude, I need to meet her. We can't let her leave before I meet her."

"Holy shit, dude," I snap back, "there will literally be seventeen women waiting outside after the game. You can choose whichever one you want, if you need to get your dick wet."

"It's not only about sex, I really just want to meet her. You know the social media girl. Send them a note. Tell them we want to have dinner with them after the game. I'll even put on a clean shirt."

I roll my eyes. "Wow. Really pulling out the big guns with a clean shirt. Yeah, okay, two more goals and I'll send word for them to join us for dinner. You got this?"

He hoots and grabs my helmet, putting our heads together. "Hat trick, coming up, boss!"

We head back out, the game tied one-one, and score just a minute into the period. I see Holly up in the box, taking photos or video with her phone. I'm sure hoping a video of the goal will be on social media. It was a beauty.

The rest of the game is fast and furious, with no more goals despite both teams taking shots-on-goal like nobody's business. About three minutes to the buzzer, we go on a power play. Chalamet gets the puck, fakes a shot on goal which sends the LA defensemen scrambling while I grab and go, skating like my life depends on it, taking a shot that looks like it will sail above the rim. It doesn't though, it drops in over the head of the goalie, and there we have it—another hat trick.

Coach pulls the line and sends in Mikhail and another rookie to play the last two minutes. They play well together, Mikhail a lot more controlled than usual as he scores his first goal in the NHL.

I grab an usher who stands nearby and ask her to write a note to Holly Laurent in the owner's box, asking her and her friend to hang around the west entrance after the game so Georg and I can take them to dinner. She grins and agrees, tells me good game, and heads off.

Six wins into the pre-season and the Crush are looking good to hold the top spot in the league as the real season begins. We are a loud, obnoxious bunch of animals in the locker room after the game. Max comes down and huddles us all together. He gives another speech about how proud he is of all of us, of how exciting our team has been to watch this season.

"Keep it up," he says loudly. "And without further ado, I wanted to announce your co-captain for this year, and team captain for next year, is...Evan Kazmeirowicz. Evan is our leading scorer this season, and he is leading us to the cup. Congratulations, Evan!"

Everyone hoots and hollers, slapping me on the back. Georg grins ear-to-ear and says, "Congratulations, asshole. Did you get us a date?"

"One track mind, much?" I ask, smiling broadly. "I sent word to them. Let me check my phone."

The other guys head off to the showers and there are several texts awaiting me. I start with my agent.

Scott: Good game tonight. Congrats on being voted co-captain. You fucking rock.

Evan: Thanks, man.

Scott: Fiona let me know that Kacey King's request had not been approved. Bad blonde.

Evan: Meh. No stress. Just won't take her word for shit in the future.

Scott: She wants you.

Evan: Ya think?

Scott: Nothing wrong with tapping a hot one.

Evan: You just want to live vicariously through me since you're married.

Scott: I've got a hot wife. No need.

Evan: Ha. Okay. Gotta run.

Scott: See you at the farm on season opener.

There are two texts from Kacey, which I delete without reading. I move on to the text from Holly.

Holly: Holy cow, you were on fire tonight! Congrats!

Evan: I was thinking about men looking at you. You look gorgeous. It made me mad.

Holly: Bc I look gorgeous?

Evan: No, bc other men see you like that and want you.

Holly: Don't be a caveman. Besides, they were all pining over my friend Pam.

Evan: Did you get my message? Georg and I want to take you and Pam to dinner.

Holly: I don't know…

Evan: Just dinner. No big deal. Georg will be heartbroken if you say no. He's even putting on a clean shirt for the occasion.

Holly: Well, in that case…

Holly: Hey Evan, it's Pam. We're IN!

I grin and head to the shower.

TWENTY MINUTES LATER, I'm in a crisp, button-down shirt, dark jeans, and a jacket. Georg, as promised, has put on a shirt that appears clean and somewhat free of wrinkles. He's got on jeans and dress shoes, and he's even pulled his hair back into a man-bun.

We head out to the west entrance and find Pam and Holly waiting. Holly smiles broadly when she sees me, her cheeks turning an adorable shade of pink. I walk right up to her and lean in, planting a kiss on her cheek before reaching down and taking her hand in mine. She doesn't pull away.

"Georg," I say, "This is Holly's friend, Pam."

"Pamela Jenson"—she reaches out to shake his hand—"but you can call me Pam."

He, of course, takes it and plants a kiss on it. She pulls away, smirking at him.

"So, you're the famous Georg Kolochev," Pam says. "Womanizer. Lover of alcohol. Player of hockey."

"Whoa." He puts his hand on his chest, and a mock look of hurt on his face.

"Your reputation precedes you, dude," I say. "Looks like you've got some work to do."

"I can handle myself."

Pam takes Georg's arm and says, "Let's see how you do tonight."

They walk off ahead of us, chatting easily.

"She seems comfortable with herself," I observe. "Not falling for his shit, anyway."

"She'll be fine," Holly says confidently. "She's made of iron."

"And you?" I can't resist the question because I need to know where I stand with her.

"Just the usual matter." She seems a little distant, but almost like she's fighting it too.

I can't help but wonder what it means, but I don't get to ask, as we are quickly at Pam's car, a convertible Mustang. I can appreciate this car. Holly and I climb into the back seat as Georg asks Pam to pick the dinner location. She checks and app on her phone first, making us a reservation at a place in Malibu, along the water.

Luckily, traffic isn't too bad. At my request, Pam turns on a classic rock station and cranks the volume as *You Shook Me All Night Long* by AC/DC plays. We all head-bang and sing loudly, letting loose, a good energy between us.

Dinner is amazing. We eat on a veranda seemingly hundreds of feet above the ocean. It's a really gorgeous scene. So gorgeous, I take out my phone and snap a picture of Holly as she looks out over the balcony. Again, her back is to me, only her profile visible, the picture a little hazy in the evening light.

I post it to my Instagram with no explanation and no hashtag before wandering up to stand beside her. Pam and Georg are still at the table. He's teaching her Russian cuss words. They've been flirty and loud all night.

"You doing okay?" I lean down close enough to kiss her, but I won't. "We really haven't had time to talk since we went skating."

"I'm okay," she says, looking up at me. She reaches out and touches the collar of my shirt, then moves her hand to my chest. "You look really handsome tonight, Evan."

"Thanks. You're stunning tonight, Holly."

She smiles sweetly, the weight of her palm still on my chest. I don't want her to move it away. I love the feel of her touching me. But finally, she says what's on her mind. "I had a fiancé in college. He cheated on me. I'm a little gun-shy."

"And I have a reputation. I get it." I pick up her hand and bring it to my lips and kiss it.

We stand there, looking out at the ocean, for a long time until Georg and Pam announce we are going dancing. I pay our bill, we load back up and head to a nearby club.

The place is hopping as we make our way in. We grab drinks at the bar, but as soon as they are drained, Pam takes Georg's hand and drags him out on the dance floor. I hold out my hand and Holly shyly accepts it. We make our way out into the throng of people. The bass is heavy, the music some mix of pop and electronic. It's not the kind of music I'd listen to on my own, but it has a great beat.

We start to move and it's hard not to be close. I end up behind Holly, my hands on her hips as we move together. There's a moment when it feels like no one else is around. She lays her head back on my chest, her eyes closed, her arms reaching up and around my neck. As we move, it's so sensual that I can't help but get aroused. I move one of my hands downward, letting it touch the bare skin of her thigh. She moans a little and turns to face me, so I put one hand at her lower back and the other between us, pushing her dress up discreetly, my finger brushing over the soft silk of what can only be spectacular underwear if it's over her beautiful body.

It's just a soft touch, nothing crazy, but she gasps, maybe a little surprised to find her panties wet already. She wants me as badly as I want her.

I move my hand and adjust her skirt, putting both hands on her ass, pulling her body against mine as we continue to sway to the beat. I want her to feel how hard my cock is right now. She looks up at me, her eyes wide and shining, her mouth parted. Waiting for me.

"God, those lips," I growl before putting my mouth on hers.

We kiss, our tongues intertwined, until she pulls away abruptly, her cheeks flushed bright pink even in the dark. "I—I—I need a drink of water," she stammers.

I nod, and we hold hands as we head to the bar. I order us both another drink as well as her water. We find a little booth being vacated and grab it. We sip our drinks and catch our breath. I peer out at the crowd and find Georg and Pam smiling and laughing, having a grand old time together.

I turn to look at Holly and when we lock gazes, it's electric. I lean in and brush my lips against hers, only to have her climb onto my lap, straddling me, her kisses furious and hot on my lips, my neck. I return the attention as she rubs herself against me. I wish we didn't have this barrier of clothing between us. I wish we weren't in a public place. I want her naked and moaning my name as I make her come. Repeatedly.

But public places are just that, and I can only dream about the time when I can really have her alone. We alternate between the dance floor and this semi-private booth all night, until last call, when Georg and I grab a taxi back to the team's hotel, and Holly slides in next to Pam in the Mustang. Her lips are swollen from my kisses and I fucking love it.

I don't know what she's done to me, but I can't get enough.

NINETEEN

HOLLY

"So...you and Evan seemed cozy last night," Pam remarks from the doorway. Her attempt to casually bring up the topic is terribly lame, but I love her for trying.

I'm packing up my things. The team is headed to San Jose for the third game in this away series—our last of the pregame season. I feel my cheeks get hot and shake my hair, so it covers my face as I stuff clothes in the bag. I have to get on the bus with the team in about two hours and I am mortified. How can I face him this morning, after throwing myself all over him last night? I didn't have a lot to drink, but I guess it was just enough to make me loosen up, to let myself react to this insane chemistry between us. Still, I don't know how I feel about him. He seems sweet and funny, he's definitely sexy, and he makes me feel really good. But pictures don't lie—he's been with lots of women in the past. And I still can't date a player without losing my job.

"Not talking to me?" Pam asks, interrupting my thoughts. "Or are you over there overanalyzing things like you always do?"

"The latter," I admit, "I feel a little slutty. Well, a lot slutty. I crawled into his lap, Pam. I might as well have had sex with him right there in the booth."

"Oh, come on! Did you notice how many people were getting it on in that place? It was like a den of sin."

"That does not make me feel better when I have to work with him. I have to be on the team bus with him today! How can I face him?"

"You think he's sitting around thinking about how slutty you are?" Pam shoots back. "No, he's not. He's thinking how much he wants a second go with you. You didn't do anything other than make out, and mostly just kissing."

"And humping," I say with a rueful smile. "I humped the shit out of him in that booth, and his hands got to be very good friends with my ass."

She giggles. "I'm totally jealous of you right now, Holls, but the important question here is do you like him?"

I nod. "I do. I can't explain it because I just don't know him that well, but I really do like him and it scares the shit out of me."

"Wow." Pam looks shocked. "You've said *shit* twice in under a minute."

"Shut up," I laugh, because she's right. Sometimes I take myself far too seriously. I need to just chill and move forward.

After Pam drops me off at the hotel I climb the steps onto the luxurious Mercedes charter bound for San Jose. I sit near the front, expecting Fiona or one of the other media team members to sit with me, but instead, Mr. Happy Hands plops down in the seat beside me.

"Good morning," he says as he shoves his backpack under the seat in front of us.

"Um, hi?"

He looks at me with a grin. "Was that a question?"

I flush hotly. Stupid cheeks always giving me away. "Hi. Good morning."

Fiona comes on the bus then, stopping to give us both a pointed look. She purses her lips and gives a snooty-sounding sniff but doesn't say anything else. She does, however, sit in the seat across from us. Presumably to make sure we keep things professional.

Evan is adept at managing things like this, though. He turns and engages her in conversation about the plan for media at the home season opener next week. I'm actually really thankful for it. They pull me into a strategy conversation, and we get some good planning done. Fiona seems less concerned about my proximity to Evan after that, even moving to go back and sit with Chalamet, claiming she wants to loop him into the media plan.

"Nicely done," I say.

"Thanks," he says, pulling a water bottle out of his bag. "That was one hour. What to do with the next four?"

I giggle. "Not what you're thinking."

"I was thinking we could play I Spy. What were you thinking? Dirty mind."

I nudge him with my elbow and he reaches over, taking my hand in his. He leans to the side and whispers, "I can't stop thinking about you."

My breath hitches and my voice sounds hoarse as I say, "Same."

"So, we do have all this time," he says softly, "let's talk."

"About what?"

"Life. You. Me." He shrugs. "Let's get to know each other a little. I'll start. What's your favorite color?"

"Green," I say, looking up at his crystalline green eyes, "like your eyes."

He blinks and bats his eyelids playfully. "Well, then, mine is brown."

"Nobody's favorite color is brown, Evan."

He chuckles. "I think my favorite color is blue. Never gave it much thought, though. What's the furthest you've ever run?"

"Marathon distance, about twenty-six miles."

He whistles his disapproval. "No thank you."

116

"Well, I wouldn't like getting slammed around while trying to stay upright on bladed shoes, so..."

He chuckles. "Fair enough. What's your fastest mile?"

My fastest single mile ever was a sub-five," I say proudly. "I usually run five to five-and-a-half on pace."

"Wow," he says, looking both shocked and impressed, "that's really fast. You never thought about running after college? Like, Olympic trials or something?"

I shake my head. "No, not really. I liked competing, but I didn't want it to be a career. I really liked my college classes and internships. I was looking forward to moving on from the sport. Now I just run for fun and to relieve stress." *And sexual tension.*

"Well, I guess I should be glad. You might not be here right now if you'd chosen a different path," he says with a squeeze to my hand.

"You played in the Olympics, though, right?"

He nods. "I did."

"In Sochi? Did you play with Georg?"

"No, he played for Russia. I played for Ukraine."

"Ohh, a little rivalry?" I ask, nudging his shoulder.

"Nah, we had a good time in Sochi." He cringes a little. "Probably too good, to be honest."

"Oh," I say, my stomach turning a bit. I pull my hand away under the guise of checking my phone. "I've got to get some work done before we get to San Jose."

"Don't do that," he says, reaching for my hand and clasping it in his again.

"What?"

"Pull away," he says, "don't let whatever you think you know about me come between whatever this is between us."

"Well, what is it, Evan? I mean, we had fun last night, but..."

"But what? We've had fun every time we've communicated. We had fun skating. We had fun last night. But I'm not just looking for fun, Holly."

"I'm not—I just don't—"

He leans in, his breath hot on my ear as he asks, "You don't what?"

I feel his nearness all the way through every cell of my body. I have to take a steadying breath before I can even speak. My voice is low and my eyes are closed when I say, "I don't know what you're looking for. I'm worried I'm not the girl for you."

"You've said that before," he says. "What's that rubbish?"

"It's not rubbish though, I'm not into casual sex. I'm embarrassed at how I behaved last night."

"Why would you be embarrassed? Why are your eyes closed? Seriously?"

I open my eyes, ready to cry for some dumb reason. I find Evan looking at me with a mixture of amusement and concern. He probably thinks I'm a total crazypants. I meet his gaze and he gives me a lopsided grin.

"We'll have to finish this conversation when we're alone *again* because that's happening. And for the record, I love how you *behaved* last night with me. But if you don't believe anything else, please believe I really like you, Holly. Okay?"

He pats my knee and says he needs to catch up with Chalamet. He gets up and makes his way to the back of the bus. Fiona returns, giving me a narrowed stare that I pointedly ignore as I check our social media feeds.

Evan comes back near the end of the trip, but we don't talk much, especially not with Fiona holding court in the seat across from us. I hope I sound professional when I wish him luck in the game. He disembarks, and I wait for the players to get off the charter before I do.

Fiona is on her phone as the media team gathers. She makes a hand gesture that tells us all to hang around. I watch Evan shoulder his bag and walk off toward the arena. Almost as if he knows I'm watching, he turns his head and gives me a sexy wink. Georg turns his head, then, and gives me a goofy grin and a thumbs-up.

Max Terry wanders up, the team's owner, and pulls on my ponytail. "This ponytail looks familiar," he says, grinning.

I blush so hard I can feel it in my hairline and my toes at the same time. He's smiling, so I'd guess he's not too bothered. Fiona, on the other hand, finishes her call, levels me with a stare that's as sharp as a blade.

"Yes. It. Does," she says.

"It's not...we're not..." I stammer.

Max pats me on the back, still smiling. He looks at Fiona and says, "Don't rock the boat, dear! Look at Tom Brady and Gisele Bundchen. That relationship was nothing but good for Tom's career. Women love a family man."

"Family man?" I ask. "I'm not even—"

"So, what you're saying," Fiona interrupts primly, "is that we're supposed to flout our no-fraternization policy in order to capitalize with our female audiences?"

"I'm just...going to go work on some...stuff," I say weakly, "it's not really...like that...with Evan."

I pull out my phone and try to focus on our Instagram feed, but Max is not finished apparently. "Look, I know Evan pretty well and I think this is the real deal. He's on fire right now, and more importantly we need to keep him on fire as we head into the season."

"Well, you're the owner, but I just think..." Fiona starts.

"Don't over think," Max says, interrupting. "Just let them be."

I look up at him, my face surely the color of a tomato by now. He winks and strolls off, whistling.

I don't see him again until we're up in the box setting up pre-game media. Fiona hasn't spoken to me since Max's endorsement of this relationship, whatever it may be, but that's honestly not any different than any other day. Max, however, sidles up next to me as I'm getting shots of the team as they do their practice drills.

"You really don't have to worry about her," he says as he looks out at the ice. "Her bark is worse than her bite."

"She's just being careful," I say. "Policy is policy."

"Very diplomatic," he says. "I'm sure there's more to it than that, but either way, it's my team. I like the idea of you two together."

"For press?" I ask casually. I continue snapping shots, trying to hide the fact my heart is about to beat out of my chest.

"I mean, sure," he says, "but moreover, Evan's a good guy. You seem like a good girl. I think the two of you might like each other and I'm a sucker for a good love story."

"It's not like that," I say for the fifty-billionth time, it seems. "We've just talked a few times by text, hung out once or twice. It's not a big thing."

"Well, little things sometimes turn into big things. Sometimes we just need the barriers to come down."

I look over and find him smirking. He nudges me with his shoulder. "Okay," I say with a tentative smile. "Message received."

We both look out at the ice and find Evan staring up at us. I give a wave and Max points to me before giving an "okay" sign with his hand. Evan raises his hockey stick enthusiastically and blows me a kiss.

"Did he ask you for permission to break the policy?"

"I'll never tell," he says with a smile.

Max heads off to talk to some VIP guests and I go down into the stands to get live video for our social media feeds as the Crush head back into the tunnel and the pre-game media begins their coverage.

It ends up being a crazy game, a fight to the finish. Evan scores one goal in the first period, has two assists in the second, and scores again in the third, with the San Jose team matching every goal our team scores. I find myself screaming and yelling, rather than working, several times, the game is so close.

The rookie Mikhail gets the game-winning goal just fifty-seconds before the end of the third period. As the buzzer goes off, I feel such elation. It really feels like they are "my" team.

I call Troy from the stands. "Did you see the game?" I ask breathlessly as he answers.

"I did," he says. "What an exciting game!"

"I know, right? Holy cow!"

"Sounds like I've made a hockey fan of you, then?"

"Totally," I say. "And more than that, I'm a Crush fan. They are so exciting to watch."

"And maybe one of them is more than that?" he asks.

"What?"

He chuckles. "You think I don't know what you look like, Holly-dolly? I've known you since you were a baby. I know that head of hair from any angle, and I know it was you on Evan's Instagram."

"I do kind of like him," I admit.

"Does it affect your job?"

"Max Terry says no," I answer, "but Fiona is not on board."

"Well, he is the owner. Just be careful will ya?"

"I know, and I will be, uncle Troy."

"Good. How's everything else?"

As I walk back up to the box to get the rest of my things, we talk some more about my job, his recruitment schedule, and the upcoming All-Star voting. After we finish our call, I finally take a breath.

As soon as I do, my mind goes straight to Evan. I want to see him. It's like Max's endorsement of the two of us has opened the floodgates of my desires to come rushing forward.

I cannot wait to be alone with him again.

TWENTY

EVAN

I puff out my cheeks and let out the breath I've been holding.

Why am I so nervous? It's not like I haven't gone out on a date before.

As I pull in front of Holly's condo, though, I realize it's been awhile since I've been this invested in someone. Actually, I don't ever recall feeling this way about any other girl. I suppose that should scare me, but it doesn't. So, I guess these nerves are more about excitement? I don't know. I suck at feelings.

I grab the bouquet of flowers from the passenger seat as I get out, practically running up the walkway to her front door. I count to twenty before she opens after I knock.

It would be a cliché to say she takes my breath away, but she does. Her hair falls in long waves over one shoulder. The evening sun bathes her in golden light, further emphasizing her bronze skin, her shoulders on display in a simple, short, blue sundress. Her feet are bare, her toes painted light pink.

"Hey," she says, her cheeks flushing pink to match her toes.

"Hey to you," I say with a grin. "You look lovely tonight."

"You too?" It comes out like a question, like she's not sure if she should say I look lovely. I'm just in jeans and a button-down. Not sure I qualify on the level she does. She giggles lightly and says, "I mean, you look handsome."

"For you." I hold out the bouquet which she shyly accepts.

"Thank you, Evan. They're so beautiful. Please come in." She presses a sweet kiss to my cheek once I'm inside. I can smell her perfume mixed with the wonderful scent that is Holly when she leans in close for the kiss. She smells like heaven, and it only makes me want to give her a real kiss with mouths and tongues, but I don't push for anything more than she wants to give me. Sometimes being a gentleman sucks, but strangely I want to take my time with her. We are in no rush.

"Do you want a quick tour of my humble abode?" She tilts her head adorably in question.

"Lead the way, Miss Laurent, and I will follow." She finds my answer amusing and rewards me with a soft laugh. I'm letting her take the lead on this, and so when she reaches for my hand to clasp with hers I grin like an idiot. But also, one big happy fucking idiot. I get the Holly Tour and the pleasure of touching her at the same time.

Her condo is fairly small, but nice. Comfortable. She's got every room painted a bright color, starting with the blue of her entryway. Her living room flows into a green color, which flows into her cheery, yellow kitchen. None of the colors are off-putting. They're vibrant, like she is. I find myself having a hard time caring about the space though, because I can't take my eyes off her lips as she speaks. I could stare at her lips for a long time.

"What's your place like?" she's asking. "I had a dream you lived on the Strip in a big penthouse in one of the hotels. It had all these windows and looked out over the city."

I meet her eyes and she blushes again. It makes me want to kiss her senseless.

"Why are you blushing?" The need for an answer is real.

"I just…"

"Because you had a dream about me?" I feel a lopsided grin take over my face. "Was it a sexy dream?"

"It was...ummm..." She looks down at her feet and flexes a few of her cute pink toes.

"So, it *was* a sexy dream."

"It was...ah...a little sexy," she admits. Her whole face is red now.

We're in the stairwell to see the upstairs. She points out the small, spare bedroom. It's the only room that's a sort of dull color, taupe or beige or whatever. She says she left it neutral in case guests sleep better in a calmer space. I'm about to ask what that means, but I get my answer as we head into her bedroom. The walls are a bright turquoise. The bedding is white. There are pops of orange in the artwork and pillows. It's a cheery, bright space and I want nothing more than to strip her naked and see that tan skin of hers spread out upon the white bedspread.

"I didn't mean to embarrass you," I say. "Your bedroom is very nice."

"Thanks. The master bath is here," she says with a gesture to a well-sized bathroom.

I peek in and make note of the huge stand-up shower with its double shower heads. Shower sex is now officially on my mind. "Nice place you've got here," I say, clearing my throat. "And you're not too far off, actually. I do live on the Strip, but in a building, not in a hotel. And it's just a normal, two-bedroom place, not a big penthouse."

She nods, pushing her lips together. "Why the Strip? Isn't it loud? Bright? Hard to relax?"

I make a face and consider the question. "I mean, it's bright, sure, but that's what blackout curtains are for. And I can sleep through a hurricane, so the noise doesn't bother me."

"Heavy sleeper?"

"Yeah," I say, "always have been."

"That's good. Do you like living on the Strip?"

We head back down the stairs as we talk. "It's fine, I mean it's been fun."

I don't want to elaborate. I specifically moved into my apartment because I figured it would be a good location for partying. Georg lives in the same building. Our neighbors are a raucous, young crowd, and I've done all kinds of things I'm not proud of in that apartment. I'll probably never have her over, just because I can't stomach the questions and doubt I know I will see in her eyes. *How many women have slept in that bed?* No. And I don't want her focused on the past. I want her to see that I'm here because I'm interested in her and only her.

She leads me to the kitchen, where she's clearly already been working on something. Without asking, she pulls two beers from the fridge, pops them open and hands me one. We clink them together before she heads to her phone and puts on some music, which blasts from a Bluetooth speaker hidden somewhere.

The music is kind of blues-rock. It sounds kind of familiar, but I can't place it. I must be making a "figuring it out face," because Holly says, "It's The Black Keys."

"Oh," I say dumbly. "It's good."

"They are good," she says, "taking a break currently, to my great dismay. I thought you might like them since they sound a little more classic than a lot of current bands."

She blushes at this for some reason, and I realize she put a lot of thought into this moment. What kind of music I might like...

"So, your parents aren't in the picture?" I ask. "Just your uncle Troy the scout?"

She nods kind of vaguely as she chops up some tomatoes. "It's fine. They raised me, gave me every opportunity. The way I see it, they both deserve to go and do their own thing. And I do have Troy. He never got married or had a family so he sort of adopted me. And we do just fine together."

"You don't seem scarred by it or anything." And she really doesn't appear to let her parental issues weigh on her, and I respect this a lot. "I was definitely a shit about things for a while when my mom and dad split up. It's one of the reasons they put me in boarding school."

She laughs at this. "I can see that. You are a little ornery."

"Tenacious," I say, grinning. "It's a good quality. What about friends? You left them all in California?"

"Pretty much," she says with a shrug. "I'm a bit of an introvert, if you haven't figured that out."

"You seem outgoing, at least at work you are. What, you don't like people?"

"Oh, I like people and I can hang, but I need lots of down time to recharge afterward, if you know what I mean?"

"Ah, yeah," I say, taking a swig of beer.

"Pam, the one you met in LA, she's my best friend. We shared an apartment my last two years at UCLA. She's two years older than me, already has her physical therapy license."

"Pam was a riot that night. She and Georg seemed to hit it off."

"She is very outgoing," Holly says, pushing her lips together in a weird little grimace-smile.

"I sense a story there," I say.

"She's wonderful and I love her, but we are very different people."

"A diplomatic answer."

She lets out a little laugh. "You're not the first person to tell me that recently. Guess my communication degree paid off."

"What else do you like to do? I know you run, and you work your ass off as social media goddess for the team. What else?"

She lifts one shoulder. "I like to cook. I like to read. I write a little, when inspiration strikes. I like listening to music. I don't know, I guess I'm kind of boring."

"I don't find you boring at all. Not one little bit."

We lock eyes and I can feel the charge, there. It's something new for me, something far more powerful than just sexual attraction, though there is that, as well.

Her cheeks flame with color, something I've come to adore about her, and she goes back to her dinner preparations, tossing pasta into a pot of boiling water.

"So, what's for dinner, Chef Beautiful?"

My comment earns me another smile and a fresh blush before she answers. "Um, I've been perfecting this very simple pasta dish for some time now. Homemade noodles, fresh tomatoes and mozzarella."

"You made the noodles?"

"Yep, and the cheese," she says proudly.

"Wow. I just, you know, open a package of frozen-something and nuke it.

She grins. "What about you? You play hockey, lived overseas, and like classic rock. What else?"

"Well, I like to work out, which seems work-related, but I do actually enjoy it."

"I like to work out, too. Do you like to just work out in the gym? Or do you like other things? Like hiking or kayaking or whatever? Do you play other sports?"

Her voice gets a little animated and I find myself distracted by her lips again. Those lips of hers will be the death of me I'm sure. I'll admit I've gone there before, and more than once. Yes, the dirtiest, filthiest place my depraved mind can go. Holly's luscious lips wrapped around my cock. Just imagining it sends me into crotch adjustment territory. I take a long swig of beer to quell the filthy images swirling in my corrupted brain, so I can answer her properly.

"I play a little pickup soccer in the spring and summer sometimes. Basketball with the guys. I'm not terribly outdoorsy but I'm also not opposed to doing outdoorsy things."

"I actually really like hiking and kayaking" —she pauses for dramatic effect— "that was a leading question in case you're wondering."

"Well, maybe we can try them sometime, then. I'm game if you're there to show me the ropes."

"Do you do anything with the team's foundation?" she asks as she pulls the pasta off of the stove and dumps it into a strainer in the sink.

"I do, when they ask me. I also have my own little fund. I mostly send money back home to orphanages, and to my old school so they can give scholarships."

She turns away from plating our meals and gives me a soft smile which nearly knocks me off my feet. "That's really sweet."

"Can I help you with anything here?"

"Sure, grab the salad and take it to the table? I can follow with these plates."

I follow her instructions and take a seat. She hands me my plate and the pasta both looks and smells amazing. I inhale deeply as she grins widely. "Beautiful and she cooks. I think you're not getting rid of me anytime soon." My remark rewards me with another delectable Holly-blush.

As we eat, we talk more about how I knew I wanted to make a career of hockey.

"I mean, I probably could have pushed it with running," she says. "It just wasn't something I wanted to pursue long-term. At least, not with that kind of pressure."

"Yeah, I get it. This pasta is amazing, by the way."

"I'm happy you like it," she says shyly.

"I think I told you, I played from a very young age. And I was smart enough, I could have gone to university, but I got pegged for Olympic trials and it just grew from there. I love playing, so it just seemed natural to go with the flow, so to speak."

"Do you like the NHL?" she asks.

"Sure, it's been fun and good for my career. Do you?"

She smiles. "So much more than I ever thought I would."

We chat more about the league and the team. She has some funny stories about some of the social media stuff she's done with the other players. I share some of my funnier team stories, as well, and we're both cracking up. Everything is going well. Until my phone buzzes in my pocket.

And buzzes again.

And again.

Fuck me for not silencing the damn thing. I won't make that mistake a second time.

Someone is totally spamming me via text. I'm guessing it's Georg, drinking and wanting to go out, or there's an emergency of some sort. I don't want to look, but after the fifth or sixth buzz, I pull out my phone. I feel my mouth automatically twist into a deep frown. Kacey King.

Kacey: Where are you tonight?

Kacey: Open invitation. Come see me. I'll make it worth your while.

Kacey: I can't stop thinking about you. We're good together.

Kacey: I want to taste you. I'm ready to come for you.

Kacey: I can't stop thinking about us together. I need you.

I have to stop her now or she'll be at this all night. I type out a quick reply and remind myself to block her number the first chance I get.

Evan: Not interested. Move on.

I look up and Holly is staring at me. She's not saying anything, but I can see by her grim expression she realizes the text is probably from a woman. My face must confirm it for her, because she stands up abruptly and starts picking up dishes. She heads to the sink, turning on the water, starting to load the dishwasher.

I hop up and grab a few more dishes, heading to her side. She won't look at me.

"Holly. Will you look at me?"

She inhales and lets the breath back out. It feels like a million years before she looks up at me with those big, beautiful brown eyes. She seems to be waiting for me to talk.

"It was the reporter, Kacey King,"

"Since when does the press directly contact players, Evan?"

"She's..." I fail to find any reasonable excuse to give her.

"Just what I thought," she says, turning back to the sink.

"But I'm not into her. I told her to move on. I just said so in my reply."

"This is a mistake," she mutters under her breath.

I can't help it, then. I grab her by the waist. My mouth is on hers before I can formulate a plan. And she doesn't stiffen. Doesn't pull away. No, instead, her hands go around my neck. She's on her tiptoes. She's opening her mouth and letting my tongue slide against hers. She lets out a little moan and I pull her as close as I can, feeling her slim body against mine. I'm hard in an instant and I can't resist grinding against her in one slow thrust. I want her to feel her effect on me, and I make sure she does.

Her arms come down, and then I feel her hands on my ass, gripping me tight and hard. She even rubs herself against my rock-hard cock, bless her sweet intoxicating self. If I didn't have any self-control right now, we'd be fucking in a matter of moments.

But not like this.

I'm the one who pulls away. Only to tell her, "Whatever this is between us? It's not a mistake."

I lean in and kiss her again, this time softly, before letting her go free. "Will you give me a chance? I know my behavior in the past doesn't inspire instant trust. And it won't mean a thing if I tell you I feel differently for you than I ever have any other woman. But I hope you can hear me when I say I need a chance. I need *you* to give me a chance, Holly Laurent."

She bites her bottom lip, looking innocent yet still carrying the expression of a woman who is thoroughly aroused. She gives me a nod accompanied by a heavy breath as she looks up at me.

"Good, it's settled. Now let me help you with the dishes and I'll even let you flick water at me."

She laughs and turns the music up. This song I recognize— *Lonely Boy*—so I make a big show of dancing and being a goofball while we clean up from dinner. The Black Keys keep playing and I decide I'm downloading every song they've ever made after tonight as a slow, sexy song comes on and I can't help but pull her into my arms.

She rests her head on my chest as we start to dance. I put my face in her hair; it smells like mint.

"Thank you for dinner tonight," I say softly.

"You're welcome, and thanks for the lovely flowers."

"They're nothing. I'd give you the world, I think...if I could."

She settles back against me and we dance a little more. Eventually I move back enough to look at her. A heartbeat passes, two, and then my lips are on hers again. I could kiss her sweet lips for days.

We don't go further. I want to. God, I want to, but she's so skittish and I cannot have her believing I only want sex from her. I want the sex, yes, but I also want other things with her. I want more.

And I'm willing to wait. It's not like I can't get myself off to thoughts of her. I've done that plenty of times already. Hell, I've been doing it since the first day I laid eyes on her.

I'm willing to earn Holly Laurent's presence in my bed. And when I do, it will be something a helluva lot more meaningful than a quick fuck on a sofa or up against a wall.

For both of us.

TWENTY-ONE

HOLLY

It's our one-month anniversary. I know, I know, I sound like a teenager, counting every day I'm with him. It's really embarrassing, but I'm also just really, really happy.

Evan has a huge social media following on his own, in spite of the fact that he posted very rarely before we started dating. Mostly, his posts were re-posts of things the team did. Everything else was stuff other people tagged him in, usually women in their own suggestive photos.

Now he posts daily pictures—selfies of us together, photos of me from the side or behind. He even got one picture of me asleep on the team bus. I did not find it flattering but the caption he posted was really sweet, so I forgave him. *Sleeping Beauty.*

About ninety-percent of the feedback has been good. For the most part, fans love that he's "settling down." The male fans, in particular, think I'm his good luck charm, since he's been posting hat tricks in nearly every game this season. The team has only lost one game so far, and we lead in the league. And superstition rules in sports, so there's a lot of commentary with things like *Don't let this one go!* because they think his play is so strong because of me. That cracks me up, but whatever.

We've just won a hard-fought game at home, and Fiona has a press event packed afterward. Evan and Chalamet cover all press now, ever since the weirdness with Mikhail. They're the team captains, so it makes sense.

The turnout is crazy, with lots of questions about our team's chances of keeping up this momentum throughout the season, all-star voting, and odds on our making it to the playoffs.

"We've got great energy out there," Chalamet is saying. Our passing is crazy good this season. It's almost like we're reading each other's minds."

Evan laughs and chimes in. "I can read your mind right now, Chalamet. You want a Miller Light, a bucket of fried chicken, and a soft bed."

"Us old married guys are way too boring," Chalamet says, grinning.

"When will you pop the question, Evan?" a young reporter yells from the back of the room. She's petite and blonde and barely visible from where I stand at the side of the room.

"To Chalamet?" he asks in response. "I mean, I love the guy, but I don't think his wife would share him with me."

The room erupts in laughter. The question goes unanswered, which is great because we've been dating a month, not a year, and the idea of marriage seems really premature. I catch Evan's eye and he grins and winks. Lots of flashbulbs go off, catching the moment. I blush, on cue, and pretend to fiddle with something on my phone.

Fiona claps her hands and yells, "Two more questions. Make 'em about sports, please."

I really love her for this, even though I know she only did it because she's still annoyed that Evan and I are allowed to flout the team's very specific no-fraternization rules. But even as the last questions turn to an injury suffered by one of our defensemen in this game, I look over and find Kacey King glaring at me. If daggers could fly out of her eyes, I'd totally be dead, because she is not happy with the talk of marriage, even as far-fetched as it is.

I don't flinch away from her stare, though. I just give her a professionally polite smile, which forces her to look away and start packing up her gear.

Holly: 1, Kacey: 0.

Not that it's a competition but it sure feels satisfying to me right now.

As the press conference ends, Evan walks over and gives me a big kiss on the cheek. "I'll just go grab my bag and meet you outside?"

"Yep. Give me ten minutes to run up and post a few post-game things?"

"Sounds good."

He and Chalamet lope down the hall, ribbing each other about the marriage proposal question.

Pam calls as I'm heading up to my cubicle.

"What's up, Pammy?"

"Good game tonight, and the post-press cracked me up."

"The bit about Evan proposing to Chalamet?"

"That very thing," she says.

"It was funny, I agree. Funny but definitely awkward for the two of us. He handled it well, but unfortunately it won't stop more of the same from inquiring minds."

"He's got a career as a sportscaster or play-by-play person once he retires from the game," Pam says. "He's really a natural in front of the camera."

"He's a natural on the ice, too. He'll probably play until he can't skate anymore."

"He'll be out there with a walker," Pam jokes.

"He might be."

"Is he a natural elsewhere as well?" She doesn't even try to disguise mischief in her voice.

I snort. "Real slick."

"This inquiring mind wants to know."

"Nosy, entitled minds, you mean?" I knew this convo was coming with Pam, I just wasn't going to be the one to initiate it.

"Same difference, Holls. Come on, throw your bestie a bone here."

"Well, if you must know, we've been taking it slow."

"Slow as in..."

"Slow as in, we haven't had sex."

"What? Why?" She sounds genuinely confused. "If I had a hot stud like that, I'd have jumped his bones on the first date." Pam makes these kinds of jokes all the time but we both know she's not serious, and to be kind, I don't contradict her. She has her own issues to shoulder.

"I wanted to, Pam, I *want* to now. He is so hot, and the chemistry is totally there, but I just felt like..."

"You wanted to make sure he wasn't just in it for a quickie." She finishes my sentence for me.

"I mean, he doesn't have a good track record. And I'm skittish. So..."

Pam makes a huffy sound of annoyance. "You need to let that shit go. Everyone's got baggage. Look at me for example."

"Yes, they do, but I'm not interested in getting hurt again. So sue me."

"Well, you do like him a lot, right?" she asks gently.

"Of course, he's a great person. We really have a lot of fun together. It feels like I've known him forever."

"And he's obviously really into you. His posts about you are super swoony. The Sleeping Beauty one slayed on social.

I can't hold back a huge grin. "They are swoony, aren't they?"

"Well, I hope you decide to put out for the guy soon, because I need to live vicariously through you to spice up my own boring situation."

I roll my eyes. "Okay, love you too, you big jerk."

"I know you do," she laughs. "Love you, babe."

We hang up and I do the post-games really quickly before grabbing my backpack and heading down to the employee parking garage where Evan parks his ridiculously audacious sports car.

He smiles as I open the door and slide into the passenger seat. "It was more like twenty-one minutes," he says leaning over the center console for a kiss.

I happily oblige, enjoying the taste of spearmint gum on his tongue.

As we pull apart, he says, "I guess I forgive you."

"I'm sorry. Pam called me."

"Say no more," he says, turning on the engine. The radio blasts but it's not his usual classic rock. Instead, the Beatles' *Saw Her Standing There* plays. We both sing along as he makes his way out of the labyrinth of a garage.

"I didn't know you liked the Beatles." He grins over at me

"Everyone likes the Beatles," I say. "*Blackbird* is my favorite."

"That's a good one. I think my favorite is *A Hard Day's Night*. I like the movie too."

"Hey, you turned the wrong way for my condo," I point out.

"We're not going to your condo, beautiful."

"Oh, do I finally get to see your apartment?" He has never invited me to his place and I'm starting to get a complex about it.

"No, it's a surprise."

I try to act unbothered by the fact that it's been a month and I still haven't been to his apartment. As we pull up into the valet lane of a very fancy hotel, my annoyance fades slightly.

"A hotel? I didn't bring anything..."

"Don't worry about that. Everything will be perfect." He plants a quick kiss on my lips before exiting the car. He's around to my side and helping me out before I can blink. He takes my hand firmly in his and gives me a satisfied grin. My guy is up to something sneaky, and I have a good idea what it might be.

We're ushered inside, and Evan spends about three minutes at the desk checking in before whisking me off to the elevator and up to the thirtieth floor. When we walk into the room, I'm floored. It's very much like the sexy dream I had so many months ago. There are floor-to-ceiling windows that look out over the twinkling lights of the Strip. The sunken living space is comfortable looking, and a full kitchen stretches out to the left, leading to a window side walkway that heads into a huge bedroom with a massive bed draped in soft, luscious, white bedding.

The bathroom is huge, with a four-person hot-tub in one corner and a grotto shower in the other. There are several shopping bags sitting on a vanity, each with designer labels. Evan gives me an impish smile when I look at him, questions surely in my eyes.

"I took the liberty of calling a personal shopper," he tells me, taking both of my hands in his. "I have no idea what's in those bags."

"Evan, this is..." I don't even know what to say. Overwhelming? Sweet? Too much? I settle for, "What's all this about?"

He answers me with a gentle kiss before leading me back out to the living area, where a bottle of wine has been chilling on the coffee table. An assortment of sweet and salty treats are presented beautifully, and two candles are lit with flames dancing. It's a very romantic scene.

As Evan pours us each a glass of wine, he says, "I can't tell you how much I've enjoyed this past month, Holly."

"It's been a lot of fun, I agree."

We sit on a soft couch next to each other. Evan picks up a remote and with the push of a button, music plays. It's too loud, so he scrambles to turn it down. It's the Artic Monkeys, though, a band I absolutely love.

"Nice touch. Are you trying to get lucky, Kazmeirowicz?"

Evan grins slyly. "I'm already lucky."

I nearly choke as I take a sip of wine. "That was so cheesy."

"Thank you," he says proudly.

"This is a really nice place." I look around the room pointedly. "Have you...stayed here before?"

He shakes his head. "No. I came over and picked the room, but I haven't been here with another woman, if that's what you're asking?"

I feel a blush coming on because he saw right through me.

"So, I don't want this to get heavy," he says, pausing like he's trying to figure out how to word what he wants to say next. "I think we need to just get some stuff out in the air, you know. Just talk through it so we can move forward. What do you think?"

I stiffen a little at this. "Talking about the past is not romantic for me."

"No, it's not," he says. "But this is a neutral zone, and we're both grown-ups, and I think if we just talk about it, maybe we can set it loose. Let it go."

"Okay..." I say warily.

"I know I have a reputation. I know there are a million pictures of me with other women out there. I know I'm not known for making long-term relationship commitments. Yes, I have a sexual history. Yes, I have been tested many times and I am clean. I can't make the past any different. But I can assure you that I care about you. That I'm interested in more than sex. That I want more with you."

"I guess I've just been..."

"Gun shy," he finishes for me. "I know. You're wary, and I suppose I would be, also. But why don't you tell me what

139

happened to you. I mean, I know you were engaged. I'm assuming you have a sexual history, right?"

"Yes," I say. "I'm not a virgin."

"Okay, so it's established that we've both had sex. What about this guy? Who was this idiot who hurt you?"

"Pam and I agreed we were just going to call him Soccer Boy. You know, He Who Shall Not Be Named. But his name was Donovan. He was a UCLA soccer player. Things were hot and heavy. We moved really fast and I fell really hard. We got engaged at the beginning of my senior year."

"Your senior year?" Was he younger than you?"

"Yes, just a year," I say. "He's a senior this year."

"So, you got engaged and then..."

"And then, a month later, he cheated on me."

"You caught him?" Evan asks.

As much as I've avoided this topic I admit it feels rather freeing to finally have it out in the open. I take a deep breath and tell him the rest. "The men's and women's teams were on a tournament trip. Pam found pictures on one of the female player's social media. They were kissing, half-naked, under the covers. It was obvious enough, and when I confronted him about it after he got home, he said they'd had an on-off sexual thing going for a couple years. He'd been casually sleeping with her since before we even got together."

Evan cringes. "What the hell was he thinking?"

I shrug. "He said it was purely sexual, nothing emotional. Said he loved me and wanted to be with me."

"So, you dumped him. Good on you." Evan smiles a little and gives my shoulder a gentle nudge. "And damn good for me because if you hadn't I wouldn't have you here with me right now."

"Yeah, good on me," I answer, loving another of his British expressions. "I mean, he tried to get me to stay, but when I asked if he could be monogamous, he couldn't answer. He looked like he physically had something stuck in his throat."

"I'm very sorry, Holly." He takes my hand and I look up through my lashes to find him looking incredibly sexy and intense.

"It's fine."

"It's not fine. And I can see why you'd be shy about getting into a relationship with someone like me."

I open my mouth, then shut it again. "It's hard not to worry that it will happen again. I think I'd feel that way no matter who I dated."

"Well," Evan says, "I won't promise to be perfect, but I can promise to treat you with respect. To be honest with you."

"That's a good start. I'll make the same promise," I say, holding out my glass toward his. He gives it a clink, the cheerful sound sort of clearing all the past regrets away.

"What do you think about trying out the hot tub?" Evan asks, lightening the mood.

"I think it sounds just lovely," I answer.

He refills our glasses and we pad in. The music filters throughout the suite, which is amazing, and Evan turns it up a tad once we realize how loud the jets are.

There's a teeny-tiny string bikini in one of the bags. It's simple and gold and fits me perfectly. I'm impressed yet horrified at the price tag. I change quickly in the bedroom and then wander in to find Evan already lounging in the hot water.

The water feels amazing, instantly relaxing my muscles. I let out an involuntary, loud sigh as I sink in. Evan hands me my glass of wine, and I take a sip before setting it back on the ledge, letting my head drop back.

"I needed this," I say on a moan. "I didn't realize how tense I was."

Evan puts his wine down and turns toward me. "Come here. I'll rub your shoulders."

I do as asked, accepting the offer of a massage. He instantly finds a knot in my right shoulder.

"Ugh," I groan. "That's the spot. Right where I carry my bag every day."

"We need to get you one of those ergonomic backpacks for all your tech."

"Indeed," I manage to whisper through the attention of his magic fingers. "Oh, that feels so good. You're my hero right now."

"Only right now?" he asks, mock hurt.

"All the time, but right now especially."

"I guess I'll take that," he says with a laugh.

"You probably get massages all the time," I say.

"Our trainers are pretty good to us, yes, but our muscles get tense and beaten up out there, so we need the therapy."

"Do you like it? I mean, the violence of the game?"

"Hmmm. Well, I mean, I can't say I like violence as a general rule. But violence is a part of the game. We're all competitive. We all like winning. It can get heated sometimes, and it does push us to work harder."

"So...yes?"

"I guess so?" he says, though it comes out like a question. "It's not like I go out and pick fights on the street. It's just part of hockey culture and we mostly leave it on the ice."

"Mostly?"

"I mean..." He trails off and focuses on rubbing the tension away from my neck.

I am perfectly content to leave conversation behind and just focus on his strong hands working on my body. A sound of pure pleasure escapes from my mouth as I tip my head forward to give him access to my neck. I have no shame either, it feels too wonderful for me to care what I say.

I get lost in the feel of his fingers as they pressure the muscles in my neck and shoulders. Eventually, he pulls me back against his chest, between his legs, and he rubs my arms. I find myself getting so aroused by this simple act of touch, and I know I'm not alone, as I can feel him going hard against my back.

I arch a little, an invitation that he doesn't miss as he moves his hands to gently massage at the sides of my torso. He takes his time, his hands finally working their way beneath the thin material of my bikini top. His fingers are so gentle as he touches my nipples, cups my breasts. I let out a sigh of wanting.

Evan adjusts, pulling his hands away and untying my suit. It falls free, floating away in the water, freeing my breasts. The cold air near hot water makes them pearl into tiny nubs that beg to be plucked.

He kisses my neck as his fingers play, one hand staying at my breasts, the other sneaking down over my stomach, beneath my bikini bottom.

I'm a live wire. It's hard to decide which feels best—his lips on my neck, his fingers strumming at my nipples, or this new sensation of his fingers dipping between my folds.

When two fingers slip inside, I spread my legs wide. It's such a strange experience, trying to find a way to brace myself in the water, but it feels so good that I don't want it to stop.

Evan holds me to him. He murmurs, "You're so beautiful, Holly. Turn around so I can look at you."

I stand, shimmying out of my bottoms as Evan pulls off his trunks. He pulls me to him so that I'm straddling him. His erect cock rubs between my legs, against my swollen clit as his lips find mine. He holds me so close, both arms wrapped around me, one hand on my lower back, one at my neck. The feeling of being this close to him, skin on skin, the water bubbling around us. It makes me feel like I might catch fire.

We kiss for a long time until Evan stops suddenly with a lusty groan. He stands up, holding me to him, and steps out of the water. Still dripping wet, he carries me to the bed and lays me down. I'm bare to him for the first time.

Evan's eyes travel the length of my body, his pupils dark, his gaze smoldering. My wet skin erupts in gooseflesh. I take a moment to revel in his naked body, as well. Wide shoulders, thick, dark hair on a sculpted chest. Washboard abs. Muscled thighs. And a cock the likes I've never seen before. It juts proudly as he stands there for me to look my fill of him. He is a beautiful man.

I sit right up on the bed and move toward him, determined to have what I want.

I take him in my mouth.

Evan's eyes close and a dirty word escapes his lips in a rush of air. I explore him, my tongue taking in the taste of skin and salt and chlorine from the hot tub. I cup his balls and slide his length down my throat. I get lost in the moment, happy to pleasure him, happy to taste the salty pre-cum that falls on my tongue.

"My turn, baby." He tells me before pulling himself out of my mouth and pushing me gently back down onto the bed again. He kisses every part of me, my forehead, my cheeks, my lips, my neck. His beard is soft and wiry against my skin. His tongue finds my nipples, licking and sucking, as his fingers again find my entrance, slipping inside, pumping lazily as my hips move to meet them.

He kisses my belly and my public bones. His tongue finds its way down to my clit, so sensitive and swollen. He bites a little, a feeling that reverberates into every nerve I have as my hips fly off the bed. He chuckles, the sound rumbling against my sex as he presses me back down into the mattress. Pinned down by his superior strength, I'm utterly devoured. He has me opened up for his pleasure and completely at his mercy. I never want it to end.

I feel myself moving up, up, up to the edge of a cliff. He's made me feel this way before, but always half-clothed. Never skin-on-skin, never like this. I want him closer—need him closer.

"Inside," I breathe. "I need you inside me."

"Only after I feel you come."

His fingers pick up the pace while his tongue continues to work at my clit. He sucks and bites and agitates and it doesn't take long for me to fall. I let out a sound that's practically inhuman as I forget to breathe, my body flexing toward the ecstasy as my insides clench and pulsates around Evan's fingers and his tongue. I hear him saying words to me, but I couldn't say what they are. I'm lost to the primal utterly and completely.

I'm not even sure I could tell him my name as I come down from the explosive orgasm he just gave me. My whole body is still primed as I watch him roll on a condom. His eyes are wild as he mounts me, ready to take us all the way. His movements firm, he stakes down my wrists with one hand and my jaw with the other. I moan as he presses the tip of his cock into me, flexing my hips as much as I am allowed. I might die like this and I don't care.

And then, he thrusts hard into me and fills me deep. We both shout as he sinks himself all the way, our bodies flush. He pauses and kisses me in the same deep and claiming way. Cock, tongue, hands all owning me at once. It's the best sexual experience of my life.

And then he starts to move. Long sliding drags in and out of my sex, hitting my clit with every excellent stroke. It takes no time before I'm coming a second time.

Just like that. He moves, and I'm gone, my body totally his, totally wired to please and be pleased. He keeps drilling me with his hard-as-steel-cock as I orgasm, pulling us closer together until there is no delineation between our bodies. He changes his position and pulls my legs up, giving him the deepest angle possible. Which he takes full advantage of as his thrusts grow even deeper and harder.

His tongue finds mine again as he continues to ride me. He kisses me as sounds of pleasure escape my throat. I feel him pick up the pace as he pushes me toward yet another precipice. It can't be possible, but I am far past the ability to do anything but be carried along for the impending climax. When he buries his head at my neck, I feel him tense, my pussy clenching in uncontrollable spasms that seem to go on forever, milking his orgasm as I come with him. The sting of pain that accompanies the end only adding to the pleasure when I realize it came from his teeth on my shoulder. Evan is wildly dominant during sex.

Please and thank you.

I don't want him to go anywhere, so I wrap my arms around him, letting him recover where he fell, along the length of my body, his cock still deep inside of me. We breathe together for minutes without saying anything. I don't think there are words to express what that just was between us, so I'm completely content to be quiet.

Finally, he does roll off me in order to pull off the condom. But he comes right back to sprawl at my side, his magic fingers back to stroking over my breasts, forcing my nipples into hard peaks again.

"God, you're so amazing," he says, kissing the spot on my shoulder where he nipped me. "You'd tell me if I was too rough with you, right? I don't ever want to hurt you, but I think I got a little carried away. I'm sorry if that was too much." His handsome face looks worried as his eyes do a thorough check of my body.

"You were perfect in every way, and I wouldn't want you to do anything different, Evan." I hold out my arms for him and he returns to lay his head on the pillow beside mine. We stare at each other, quietly relaxing, touching hands, breathing.

I am the first to speak. "Well, that whole plan really worked out for you, didn't it?"

We both burst into laughter. "Well, I hoped it would, but I would've settled for another night of making out with your very kissable and intoxicating lips."

"This was so much better than making out though. Thank you for setting up our first shag, as the Brits say. Do you ever call it that?"

He laughs at my question and just shakes his head at me. "You're welcome for the shag-party, darling. When can we do another?"

"If you feed me maybe sooner than you think," I tease him right back.

"Oh shit, yes. Can I order us something? Or do you want to go out for a bit?"

"I'm never leaving this room, so I guess we'd better order in," I say with a smirk. "I think staying in will be much...more enjoyable for the both of us."

The implication is heavy in the air. In fact, the air is thick with this deepened connection between us, so much so that I find myself ready again, the pool of want swirling hot in my belly.

Evan gets up from the bed and leaves the room as I enjoy the sight of his tight ass flexing as he walks out. He's back in mere moments, this time with the wooden board from the coffee table piled with fruit, cheese, bread, and other delights. He holds it low on his hips, so I can't view his important bits. He's so cute right now I could die.

"My woman wants food? I deliver."

"How very caveman of you, but I'm totally into it."

He places the board on the bed beside me and climbs back in. He takes his time making me a tiny sandwich with the bread, cheese and what looks like smoked turkey, before bringing it to my mouth. He's feeding me food and my heart can't take much more of the romance or it will surely explode. My eyes are unable to look away as he feeds me bites of food. I take each bite from his careful fingers and feel like the most cherished woman in the world.

Evan takes his own bites in between mine, occasionally giving me a kiss or two to break it up. We don't speak. We are quiet and content, both of us taking our fill of each other. I look at him, and he looks at me, his eyes staring boldly wherever they will. The mood between us is inferno-hot, yet mellow at the same time.

And in this romantic way we eat what is probably the best dinner I've ever enjoyed in my life. Eventually we are full, and the tray gets moved off the bed. He's sitting up against the headboard when he gets back into bed.

I know exactly what I'm doing.

This time, I push Evan flush against the headboard and I straddle him. I rub his cock against the wetness of my slit until his length is rock hard and weeping at the tip. His hands knead at my breasts and play with my nipples; all while wearing a smirking grin on his handsome face.

"You're sexy when you smirk at me like that."

"You're sexy all the time," he mumbles.

I grab another condom and roll it along his length before putting him inside of me. Hands braced on the headboard, I ride him with a purpose. He fills me so good. I start slow, leisurely, enjoying every penetration in and out. But before long, I'm moving faster, spurred by the pinches and bites he places on my nipples with his lips and teeth. His big hands are gripping the sides of my hips and working me on and off his cock with gusto. When I come, it's maybe the most intense orgasm I have ever had. I would swear it was like nothing I've ever experienced before tonight.

We take our time after that, Evan rolling me over without breaking our joining. He slows the pace, looking into my eyes, making sure I know this is more than sex.

The connection between us is electric. It's so intense that I feel a lump forming in my throat, one I have to swallow. I feel my eyes leaking. Not in a rush, but a few tears roll down to fall on the sheets. Evan sees my tears, but kisses and licks them away, his tongue trailing down my cheek. He doesn't stop for a long time and I don't want him to. When he comes it's less intense than the first time, but no less pleasurable. I feel him inside me when I fall asleep wrapped up in his arms.

But later, in the very early hours of morning, as we both find ourselves sleepy-awake at the same time, I tell him, "I really do care about you, Evan. And I trust you."

"Thank you for telling me that." He brings a finger to my lips and traces over them with the softest touch. "It means everything to me, Holly."

I curl up in the crook of his arm, sleep taking over once more.

I'm almost asleep when I hear him.

I can't be sure I heard him correctly either, but it sounded like, "I don't know what you've done...to me...Holly...*ruined*...me for anyone else."

Ruined, really? I couldn't be totally sure that's what he said, though. Between his accent and my sleepy state, I could have heard a lot of things.

Evan seems to sense my worry and pulls me in a little closer. I hear him speak one word, this time as clear as a bell.

"Crushed."

I smile as I drift away.

TWENTY-TWO

EVAN

W ho has two thumbs and got voted in as Pacific division starting winger for this weekend's All-Star games? This guy.

Okay, that didn't work out as well as I thought it might. Just imagine me pointing my two thumbs at myself.

Whatever. I'm psyched.

Did I mention I'm also one of four captains for this rave-up? Yep. El Capitan. That's me.

And the icing on the cake? Georg got voted onto the All-Star team. I was honestly shocked, because Georg is a bit of a wild-card and has a smaller fan base than some other players have. However, he's been on fire this season and his play has been way above-average, so there is no arguing he's right for the job.

Because there are two of us from the Crush, Fiona sends the media team to follow us through the weekend. There are skills competitions and three-on-three matches. It's going to be a total blast.

What the average person needs to know about All-Star weekend is that it's basically fantasy football made real. And with hockey. There are four teams—Pacific, Central, Atlantic, and Metropolitan. They're made up with players selected by fan voting, which creates a sort of "dream team" effect that fans geek-out on.

We're in Los Angeles for the big weekend, and I'm having breakfast with my agent, Scott, who's beyond stoked that I'm having such a crazy good season so far.

"I don't know what Kool-Aid you've been drinking, my man, but it has turned you into a superhero," Scott says as he stabs at his omelet.

"Got a lucky charm," I say, grinning and giving a side-eye to Holly, who sits at another table with Georg and her friend, Pam. Georg's hair is wild today, and not pulled back in his usual man-bun or ponytail. Pam's hair, blonde and thick, hangs loose around her shoulders. It occurs to me these two would make a very nice couple. I look back at Scott, who's sipping form his coffee mug.

"Well, I hope it stays that way," he says with a tiny bit of a grimace. I don't think it's because the coffee's too hot.

"What was that face?" I ask.

"What face?"

"The barely-there grimace telling me you aren't super on board with my off-ice happiness."

"No, not the case," Scott says, shaking his head. "I am happy for you. It's just...you're you. And this has gone on like seventeen times longer than any other moment of happiness you've had. So, I worry it's about time you'll kick her to the curb."

"First," I say, sticking a piece of bacon in my mouth, "That's rude. And I'm hurt."

Scott makes a face which tells me he isn't buying it.

"Look, she makes me happy. I care about her. I can't explain why it's different, but it is."

"It's not because you're scoring a ton and the fans love your little romance? Or because the two of those things together probably got you your spot on the All-Star team?" He shakes his head in the negative. "Look, I understand using a thing to your advantage. It's working for you. But you'll have to stop pretending at some point, and I'm worried about that little girl, because I think her feelings are real."

"Oh, now you're the expert on feelings?" I'm actually kind of hot about this right now. At first, I was willing to take a ribbing, but now I feel like he's going over the line.

Scott puts up his hands. "I'm sorry," he says.

I lean in and say, "Scott, I like you, but if you ever shit on my relationship with Holly again, I will fire you."

Scott's mouth folds into a line and he gives a short nod. "I'm sorry," he says again. "I really am. I can see now... this is different for you. So, great. I'm happy for you."

"Whatever."

"Seriously, man," Scott says. "I meant no disrespect. Like I said, the fans love this thing you've got going on. You seem happy. You're playing like a friggin' boss. Who am I to judge?"

We sit in tense silence for a few minutes until Scott finally breaks the ice. "So, I will say your girlfriend is a total genius when it comes to managing social media."

"That she is," I say. "She was really fair, promoting all the guys who were interested in All-Stars. She pushed me a little more once it looked like I just needed a bump over the edge. She's really smart with messaging and timing."

"It's safe to say she's got a strong career in sports marketing ahead of her, no matter what else happens." I give him a sharp look and he says, "I'm just saying, she might not want to work for the Crush forever."

I lift a shoulder. "I don't know. She's loving it right now. Max Terry thinks she's the greatest thing since sliced bread. He'd probably give her a million-dollar contract if she ever tried to leave."

"She's doing good things," Scott says. "My company asked if she was a free agent. They're looking for someone to promote the talent."

I feel my eyebrows rise into my hairline. "Really?"

He nods, his face earnest. "They said she's the best social media manager in pro sports right now."

"Damn," I say. My heart swells with pride.

"So, let's chat about the games. You know the format. We start tomorrow with the skills competition. The division that racks up the most points gets to pick which division it takes on in the semis. Sunday, you'll play the first semi-final game, and if you win, you'll go onto the finals. They're twenty-minute games with two, ten-minute halves. It's a show for the fans, so make it a good one."

"Got it," I say, though I probably know the format better than he does.

"You know, we've got major leverage to get you a killer contract negotiation this year. You're more than halfway through the season. Don't get hurt and don't do anything stupid and we'll be just fine."

"Scott, when have I ever done anything stupid?"

"Hmm. Let me think on that one," he says, checking his watch. "I've got to run over to look in on my guy at the Lakers. I'll take care of the bill on my way out."

"Thanks."

"Evan," Scott says as he stands and grabs his suit jacket from the back of his chair, "I'm really sorry. I shouldn't have been such an asshole. You're on fire this season and I couldn't be happier for you."

He holds out for a fist bump, which I oblige, but only because I'm not letting his comments ruin my mood.

As Scott leaves, I wander over and slide into the booth next to Georg. He's in full-on flirtation-mode with Pam, and Holly's engrossed in her phone, working on the team's accounts.

"How's Scott-the-agent-extraordinaire?" Holly asks idly.

"He's a bloody wanker, and other shit I can't say in a public restaurant." Holly's head snaps up, her eyes wide. I shrug. "He is. He thinks our relationship is just a thing for the press."

"Oh," Holly says, her face going dark. "That's not true, though."

"Who cares about him," I bite back. "He did also say you're the best social media manager in sports right now. His company wants to hire you to rep their clients."

Her face turns to totally shocked. "Uh. What?"

"He represents players for the NBA, the NFL...he's talking all sports, not just hockey. The best. That's exactly what he said, Holly. That you're killing it."

Pam wraps her arm around her shell-shocked friend. "Hey, girlie, look at you!"

"I wish my boss thought that," Holly mutters. "But it's nice of him to say. I still have a lot to learn."

"Don't do the humble thing," Pam says. "You're awesome. Just bask in it."

We all chat for a few minutes before Georg and I have to head out for our practice window.

"How about we all go out tonight?" Georg announces. "Maybe do a little dancing? Celebrate?"

"I'm down," Pam says.

"Sure," Holly says. "Sounds fun. But not too much alcohol, okay? I need you two feeling good for skills tomorrow."

"Yes, Mom," Georg says, laughing.

OUR PRACTICE SESSION is great. The fans picked a great group of Pacific players. There's some ribbing about various game moments, and a fair amount of good-hearted shit-talk, but we have good energy and a lot of talent. We work through our drills and leave feeling confident we'll be able to own tomorrow's skills competition.

After we finish, we head back to the hotel. The league puts All-Stars up in a much nicer hotel than during the usual season, since we're all coming in to do this extra thing for the fans, on top of our regular season duties. As a captain, I have a killer suite and all I can think about is bringing Holly back here later so we can christen every surface of this place.

I shower and dress, texting Georg and the girls the plan for dinner. We all meet up and get a car service to take us out to a restaurant in Santa Monica, one Pam says will make us all "spontaneously combust, it's so good."

In the back of the SUV, I can't help but put my hands all over Holly. She's in a tiny, electric blue dress which shows off her long and lovely legs, all the way up to her thighs. I rub my fingers along gorgeous exposed skin, and by her uneven breathing, I can tell she's just as turned on as I am. In the seats in front of us, Pam and Georg are flirt-fighting about some show she likes, and he hates. They're paying no attention to us, so I slip my hand up under her dress, pushing aside her panties and sliding my middle finger into her wet, wet pussy.

She swallows a little sound of arousal and looks at me sharply, shaking her head. I pull my finger out, not having to be told twice, but give her a naughty grin before sticking my finger in my mouth and licking it off deliberately. I lean in and kiss her, making sure our tongues intermingle before pulling away.

"See how good you taste?" I whisper, enjoying the transition as she blushes furiously.

At the restaurant, I make a point to touch her under the table as often as I can. Mostly I just touch her knee and lower thigh, but there is a moment when she spreads her legs just a little, just enough for me to slide my hand up further, to find her clit and strum it idly, all while pretending I'm hearing even one word of the conversation.

Dinner is good, for sure, but it's not the food that's ready to make me combust. It's this gorgeous woman. I want nothing more than to take her to a quiet hallway and fuck her silly. But no, the fun is in waiting. The fun is in going just so far, just far enough to make the wanting so strong we'll get lost in each other once we're back in my hotel room. I said it already, I've got plans for that suite.

"I've got a great club to show you guys," Pam says as we head back out to the car. She gives the address and our driver heads off.

It's not too far away, and we're able to skip the line because the bouncer recognizes Georg and me. "All-Stars, yo!" he says by way of greeting as he unhooks the velvet rope and stops us only for a quick selfie and a fist bump.

Inside, the club is packed. It's really cool, all decorated with a Middle Eastern flair. It has seating areas half hidden by colorful curtains and covered in patterned pillows. Georg notices none of this, going straight to the bar, but the girls gush over the design. All I can think of is the modicum of privacy which those seats provide. We could have lots of fun here, for sure.

The music's pumping and the dance floor is full of gyrating bodies. I see one, though, which makes me frown.

"What's that face all about?" Holly asks, looping her arm through mine.

I nod to the dance floor. "Viktor Demoskev."

"The guy who injured you earlier in the season?" Her face hardens.

"Yup, the very one." I turn away from her and toward the bar. "I need a drink."

We make our way over to Georg, who tries to act like he wasn't just flirting with the bartender as Pam sidles up to him. He looks at me and raises an eyebrow.

"Demoskev's here," I tell him.

"*Etot gryaznyy ublyudok*," he snarls, turning to look out. His eyes narrow as he sees the big Russian.

"Oooh," Pam gushes. "Russian. Hot."

"He called Demoskev a dirty bastard," I translate. "He only speaks Russian when he's really pissed or really drunk."

"Isn't he really drunk most of the time?" Holly asks, almost too quietly to hear.

I ignore the comment because what is there really to say about Georg's drinking? "I forgot he made the Atlantic team," I say. "I fucking hate that guy. How did he get the votes?"

"Well he's not ugly," Pam says.

"*Zatknis*'" Georg hisses at Pam. "Do not say that about him. He's a filthy piece of shit."

"I'm just saying, women probably did the voting," Pam says. "Should we find another place to go? I don't want you two getting in a pissing match. We're supposed to be having fun."

"No," I say with a sigh. "It's a free country. Let's just get a few drinks in us and go stake out one of those semi-private seating areas."

"Sounds fun," Georg says. He orders us all a round of shots and a round of beers, and we head off to the first open seating area we can find.

Holly and I clink glasses and take a few swigs of beer before I pull her close to me, my arm around her as she leans back against me. The swell of her breast is tantalizing in her strapless dress. My fingers stroke the sensitive, exposed skin and she sighs.

I kiss her neck and she lets my other hand explore between her thighs. We're somewhat hidden by the curtains and literally no one is looking at us right now. Georg and Pam are on the dance floor.

"I'm going to have you six ways to Sunday when we get back to the hotel," I say in her ear. "I've got lots of plans for you, beautiful."

"Oh yeah?" she asks on a breathless whisper. "Can I have a little preview, so I know what I'm looking forward to?"

I nod slowly in the affirmative. "I'm going to start us a hot shower. We're going to undress each other, and then I'm going to soap every inch of that perfect, luscious body. I'll take my time, maybe massage the parts of you that seem to most need my attention. I'll make you weak and boneless with want, and then I'll get on my knees and worship your sweet pink pussy with my mouth. I'll fuck you with my tongue until you scream my name. And when you do, I'll pick you up and bury my cock as far into you as I can. We won't know where I end and where you begin, we'll be so close. But I'll go slow, Holly baby. I'll take my time. I'll drive you crazy. I'll make the wanting build and build until you beg me to go faster, to take you harder. And when you come, you'll forget what planet you're on."

"I wanna go to Planet Evan right now, and I *love* it when you talk all hot and dirty to me," she says with a bit of a slur to her words. It occurs to me that my girl is maybe a little bit drunk, and I need to take care of her. Keep her safe.

Right after I make her come.

"I'll speak this way to you whenever you'd like," I growl, barely realizing I've slipped my fingers inside of her while I've been playing out this vision in my head. Her eyes are closed, the fact that we're in public completely forgotten. My thumb strums over her clit as I pump my fingers in and out of her very wet pussy. It only takes a few moments before I feel her clench around my fingers, the rest of her body shuddering in my arms as she comes. Fuck. It was so hot just watching her do that.

I lean over her and kiss her deeply before slipping my fingers free. I pull her skirt back down, and finally, press a kiss to the side of her head. She turns and throws her legs over my lap. I lean in and find her lips for a long, lingering kiss. When we pull away, she looks dreamily satisfied.

"You're getting so much more later on tonight," I remind her, reluctantly pulling myself back to reality. A few long moments pass as the two of us stare into each other's eyes. Holly blinks as Georg and Pam emerge from the light of the dance floor back to our darkened corner, breaking our little spell.

"Hey, who am I?" Georg jokingly shouts while gyrating wildly in Pam's direction to the music blaring overhead.

"I give up, G." I turn towards him as Holly straightens in the booth and blushes right on cue.

"*Did they see us?*" she mouths to me. I shake my head no.

"John Travolta," Georg answers, grinning like a motherfucker with his left arm up over his head. "I've got big

158

time boogie fever!" He spins Pam and flings his arm straight back with a jerk.

Unfortunately clocking somebody standing right behind him in the face as they near our table.

Everybody freezes, whipping eyes around onto the unlucky person Georg just slapped.

Georg discovers exactly who the unlucky bastard is at the same instant I do.

None other than Viktor Fucking Demoskev.

Standing in front of our table, a beer bottle in his hand, a girl at his side, and a slight red mark across on his face from Georg's impression of *Saturday Night Fever*. The fucker is huge, with broad shoulders and pecs so defined I can see them through his shirt. He has a wicked scar high on his left cheek, though with a reputation like his it's a miracle his whole face isn't scarred.

"So that makes her Olivia Newton John, then?" Viktor says tightly, the aggression in his stance proving he was only coming over to our booth to start some shit.

"Your mind is confused, Demoskev," Georg says sarcastically, "not surprised you don't know the difference between *Grease* and *Saturday Night Fever*, but I would hope you could've left it on the ice where it belongs, asshole."

"Fuck off, Georgie Boy." Viktor bites back.

"Watch your mouth in front of the ladies," Georg snarls.

"You mean these puck bunnies?"

"Don't talk about me that way," Pam interjects angrily.

"Let the boys chat, slut!" Viktor says dismissively, insulting Pam.

Pam is over in Viktor's face before I can even register. She jabs her finger into his chest as she releases a torrent of snarling accusations about what a Cro-Magnon moron he is. Viktor smiles at first but when he tries to flick away her finger, she pushes him. In a blur, he side-steps her and throws a wild haymaker toward Georg. It just misses his nose. Pam loses her balance and goes down in the scuffle.

I leap over the table just as Georg lands a punch to Viktor's jaw. There's a lot of swearing happening, mostly in Russian, and as I try to pull Georg away from Viktor, Viktor manages to get a punch in on me which lands squarely on my right eye. I feel it swelling almost immediately.

"Well, damn," I say, grabbing a beer bottle and smashing it over his head. He turns, blood leaking from his temple, and grabs me, pushing me back into the table. My weight butterflys the table, shot glasses and beer bottles raining down on me as I scramble to get back up, determined not to go down in this fight.

I jump up, landing a superman punch to his cheekbone, feeling it crack under my fist. He staggers backward as Georg pummels him in the stomach. When Viktor falls to the floor Georg hollers down at him, "Don't get up, *yebanko*!"

At this point, I look around for Holly and find her clinging to Pam, wide-eyed with her hand over her mouth, horror etched into her features as she scans the scene and realizes there are about seventy people surrounding us, all with their cell phones out. All the color drains from her face as she meets my gaze. Her hand goes down to her throat, and I can see her struggling to breathe. She's having a panic attack and I need to get her out of here right the fuck now.

Bouncers are trying to get to us through the crowd. As they do, they signal that we're done. It's time to go. I grab Holly's hand and make our way toward the doors, outside, to the waiting car.

It's not until we're in and belted and on our way that I am able to look at Holly. Her hands tremble as she pulls out her phone, scanning the social media feeds. "Are you okay, baby?"

"It's everywhere," she says, her voice cracking. "Your eye, Evan." She brings her fingers up to my chin, turning my face so she can assess the damage. "It's swollen up badly."

"Damn." It's all I can think of to say to her. That she's freaked out is an understatement. I'm not pleased either. This is a major fuck up for all of us.

"I'm so sorry, Georg," Pam says. "It was totally my fault. I provoked him."

"I'm just really fucking relieved you're okay," Georg says. "He started it. He said nasty things about you. And when you schooled him he made it violent. Not your fault, Pam."

"I'm going to get fired," Holly says in a soft voice. "And you guys...it's All-Star weekend. This is really bad. Really, really bad."

No one says another word the whole thirty-minute ride back to the hotel. We go straight up to my room after saying a brief, terse goodnight to Pam and Georg in the lobby.

Holly pulls a first-aid kit out of my hockey bag. She starts checking out my wounds. Scratches on my hands, a swollen and black eye, a laceration on the back of my neck. Several bruises that will require ice. I'm pretty sure my pinky might be fractured but I'm not telling her that.

"It could be worse," I say quietly.

"How? How could it be worse?" she snaps.

"I could have been seriously injured," I remind her. "This is just surface stuff."

"How in hell can you play with your eye swollen shut? Shit! Why did you get involved, Evan?"

"He insulted you and your friend, if you didn't notice," I say angrily.

"Yes, but Georg was there to defend her."

"So, Georg can get into a scrape the night before All-Stars but I can't? I'm supposed to just stand back and watch?"

"Maybe," she says. "You're a captain for fuck's sake. You're a captain for the Crush! You're their role model. This is bad for you, Evan. And for me. All those people with their phones out..."

161

"You can literally get a job anywhere else," I say. "So what if you get fired?"

"Who'd fucking hire me after they see video of me in a bar fight, Evan?"

"You weren't in a bar fight, Holly. *I* was in a bar fight. You were an innocent bystander and I was defending your virtue and your friend's virtue. We can spin it. Everyone knows Demoskev is an aggressive prick. We'll just make sure people know what he said to tip things off."

She wanders over to the kitchen and bangs the drawers open and closed until she finds a bag, then she fills it with ice from the freezer. She practically throws it at me and says, "Put this on your eye."

I don't know why this pisses me off so much. It just does. I say, "You're overreacting. For one, you're swearing an awful lot and that's not you. So just take a minute, breathe, and calm yourself."

"Don't tell me how to feel about this!" she yells angrily. "You know what? I'm leaving. I'm going to my own room, taking a bath, and figuring out what to do about this social media mess that will probably have me in the unemployment line by morning."

She heads toward the door, but I'm not letting her go so easily. No, I'm up and on her like a tiger on its prey. She spins around, mouth open to shout at me. Probably planning on telling me to go sit down, or leave her alone, but she doesn't get any of it out before my lips are on hers.

At first, she tenses, but then she opens up to me, my tongue slipping inside as I press her against the door. She bites my bottom lip hard enough to draw blood. She calls me a 'dirty fucker' much to my surprise. I kiss and bite her neck in response as I lift her dress up over her hips and pull the top down to meet it. It bunches at her waist, her tits exposed and ready for my mouth. I rip her panties off of her as she fumbles with my belt and jeans. They fall to my ankles and I'm inside of her, ramming her against the door, her legs wrapped around my waist, my cock stroking deeply as I pump into her hard and fast.

She doesn't come, but I do, and quickly. But it's fine. I manage to get us both to the couch and lay her down, so I can ravage her tits with my lips and teeth. She arches her back, spewing sharp words at me. She's so furious right now, and this is nothing but an angry fuck, but we both need it, angry or not. We need the reminder that our connection goes so much further than the clusterfuck from tonight can hurt us.

I slip three fingers inside her. It's sloppy and wet and it only gets wetter while I bite at her nipples. She moves her hips almost violently, meeting my thrusts, her face serious and determined. When she comes, her tense expression melts away her head tilts back and her eyes close. Her orgasm seems to last forever, and watching it happen is hot as fuck.

I'm hard—ready to go again as I carry her to the bedroom and lay her out on the massive bed. The rest of the clothes and shoes go away until we're both naked and I can do my best work. A soft bed and Holly naked beneath me are the sum total of my requirements right now.

I take my time kissing her, sweetly and thoroughly before moving my lips to other parts of her body that need my attention. When I have her writhing beneath my kisses and I know she's ready, I line up my cock and push inside her slowly, watching the penetration of her tight little cunt as she takes me all the way to my balls. So fucking sexy. I want it burned into my memory for the rest of time.

The satisfied moan she gives me tells me I got it right.

We make love, finding a soft rhythm totally different from the violence of just a moment ago. When we come again, I have her eyes on mine as we convulse together, our bodies so close we can't tell where one of us ends and the other begins. I keep my promise to her from earlier.

I want to tell her I love her, but I'm afraid. We need to talk this whole mess out first. But now is not the time because we're both drained and exhausted. We need sleep. And I need to clear away all the shit from tonight out of my head. And I need to hold the woman I love in my arms.

WHEN I WAKE up, I feel like I've been hit by a truck, but more worrisome to me is that Holly is nowhere to be found. There's no note, no text, no voice mail. However, my agent has spammed me with about a thousand texts telling me to call him *right the fuck now*.

I dial up as I shuffle into the bathroom to shower and get ready for the day. My eye is swollen but not as bad as expected. My pinky has turned purple. The rest of me is banged and bruised but I won't let it get in the way today. I won't let any of it get in the way.

"What the actual fuck?"

This is the way Scott answers his phone.

"Have you seen the news today?" he barks. "You and Georg are all over social, all over the broadcast stations."

"I just woke up."

"Well, to catch you up to speed," he says sharply, "the league covered your asses by paying the club owner for the damage you caused. You're welcome. You're fuckin' lucky you're not arrested for assault, and that's only because Demoskev, of all people, took responsibility for it and said he didn't want to press charges."

"Really..." I can't believe what I'm hearing.

"Yes, really. He told the police he was drunk and saying things to try to goad you and Georg into a fight. He said Georg only intervened when he insulted your dates, and you only intervened to pull Georg off of him."

"That's actually close to the truth," I say. "They both must have forgotten about Georg's accidental backhanded spin move to the face."

"Viktor's been suspended from participation in the weekend," Scott continues. "He's probably already in a press conference to say all of it on record."

"Well, sounds like it's all fine and dandy, then. Why so bent?"

"Evan," he says, calmer now, "This is not like you. Did I not just tell you we'd be fine, if you didn't get hurt and you didn't do anything stupid?

"You did say that, yes." He's right, but right now I'm more concerned about what's up with Holly.

"Are you hurt?"

"Minor things. It won't keep me off the ice."

"Fuck!"

"Demoskev made the first move," I remind him. "Georg was only having a good time with Pam. And we were in a loud, crowded club. Let's focus on that."

"I get it," he says. "I do. I really do. It's just your stock was so high, man. You were having a pretty perfect season. You were looking settled and stable off the ice. This is just not good, Evan."

"Scott, okay—I mean, what do you want me to say? It wasn't our fault. Could I have tried to diffuse it? Sure. I mean, I did, but he kept pushing."

Scott sighs on the other end of the line. "Okay, well, I've got to run. Good luck out there today."

I hang up without saying goodbye. I guess that could have been worse. Barely.

I shower and take a few Ibuprofen. I've got a few hours before the skills challenge starts, so I call for a car. The driver must know my state of mind, because the Marshall Tucker Band is playing. The song is mellow, guitar-driven, and the singer's voice is gravelly as he sings, *Can't you see? Can't you see? What that woman's been doin' to me.* I lay my head back and let the song wash over me, while I think about what Holly has done to me. I thought I was just going out for flowers, and maybe I'll stop and get those, too, but I have the driver instead take me to Rodeo Drive, where I wander into the first jewelry store I find.

A too-skinny woman in a black pantsuit greets me. "Hello, can I help you?"

"I want to buy an engagement ring," I tell her.

"Congratulations," she says with a smile, walking back behind the counter. "Come on over here and let's talk. Tell me about your girlfriend." I approach the glass case and see that her name is Candace according to her badge.

"Well, Candace, she's very stylish but also not ostentatious. She's smart and talented but also practical. She likes bright things but bigger is not necessarily better in her book. And she's an athlete, a runner."

"Okay, so I'd say let's splurge on quality rather than size. I've got a few simple designs that won't be too heavy or bulky when she's working out."

Candace pulls out a few selections and we talk about each one. I'm not feeling any of them though, so she purses her lips, thinking, and then holds up a finger and runs over to another case. The ring she pulls out is more of a band than anything else, with one larger stone in the middle of a row of diamonds that glitter all the way around the band.

"This is perfect, thank you, Candace."

I make my purchase and leave, thinking about how I think I knew Holly was the one the moment I met her.

Is it crazy I'm out buying an engagement ring? Yes. Yes it is. It's crazy because I never saw myself as the guy who would settle down and make a commitment. It's crazy because we've only been together a few months. It's crazy because I haven't even had the courage to tell her I'm in love with her.

For a million reasons, I should not have bought this ring yet. And maybe it will be a while before I give it to her. Hell, maybe she'll decide I'm not worth the risk to her career. Maybe she doesn't love me back. But the feel of the box in my hand is reassuring, for some reason, so I feel like I made the right decision, as impulsive as it was.

I feel so good about this I go into the skills competition with a fire in my belly. Georg wanders in only minutes before it's about to start. He's just as badly beaten as I am, with bruises on his face and hands.

"Did you hear?" he asks as he suits up. "Demoskev did a press conference this morning and took responsibility for the brawl?"

"I heard...after I got my ass chewed by my agent."

Georg shakes his head. "We dodged a bullet, man."

I nod. "We did. But he was a fucking shitbag who deserved to have his ass handed to him."

"True," he says. "I'm so relieved Pam wasn't hurt in the clusterfuck."

I grimace. "I suppose it's why he's so penitent. We're on camera defending women. He's on camera insulting and nearly hitting them."

We head out and take the ice. After passing, puck control, and hardest shots, the Pacific team is in the lead for points. Our goalie—a goalie from Vancouver—struggles to save the first few shots. We don't necessarily need him in order to stay ahead, but it would be nice to have the points. Plus, I need him to be able to make saves as our starting goalie.

He warms up and comes in second in the competition. The day is pretty fun, with lots of people yelling for me and Georg, most of them giving us the thumbs-up for handing it to Demoskev.

After showers, we're rounded up for press. Most of the questions are light and focused on the fun aspects of the day. I get a few about the scrap at the bar. Fiona has instructed me to say as little as possible, so all I say is, "It's really encouraging to hear Viktor take responsibility for what happened. I could have kept a more level head, too. It was unfortunate, but I'm ready to move on. Hockey is all any of us want to focus on going forward."

I check my phone a million times. Nothing from Holly, despite my numerous voice mails and text messages. I probably look like a stalker. I text her one more time: **Baby, will you please tell me if you are okay?**

We play the Metropolitan team tomorrow morning. I need to sleep. I need to ice my injuries. I need to perform well tomorrow. But even though I know these things, all I care about is finding Holly and making sure there still is an *us*.

TWENTY-THREE

HOLLY

I've been hiding from Evan's view the whole day. I know I'm being immature. I should totally just go talk to him, or at least text him to let him know I'm okay. His texts and messages sound more and more worried, and even though he's performing well in skills, I can see on his face that his head isn't totally in the game. He keeps scanning the arena and I know he's looking for me, which is why I'm well hidden in a little pocket of seats at the far end of the arena, wearing an Anaheim hat, which he would never allow. He would call it bad luck, but hey, it's good disguise.

I do feel like a traitor wearing it, for the record. That said, I was getting recognized earlier in the day and I needed to hide not just form Evan, but from everyone.

I snuck out of his room almost as soon as he fell asleep. I couldn't sleep due to the huge pit of anxiety that settled into my stomach. I needed to know what was out in the world about the fight. I needed to have a plan for how I would answer questions about it. There was also the little issue of him coming inside me sans condom. Twice. I absolutely cannot blame him for all of it, though. I was just as into the angry-sex session as he was.

Fiona's call came at five in the morning. We met for breakfast and she frowned the entire time. The conversation went about as well as to be expected.

169

"I should fire you," she said while stirring milk into her coffee.

"I didn't really do anything wrong, Fiona. Viktor was really nasty, and it wasn't until he started insulting my friend and me that the guys got involved."

"I spoke with Max earlier and he said Viktor will accept responsibility. But that's not the point. The point is that you've already blatantly flouted our rules on fraternization by dating Evan Kazmeirowicz. Then you're out with a second player and you're in the middle of a bar fight with these guys. This does not look good for the team, Holly."

"I understand it doesn't look good," I said. "Do you think I'd work as hard as I do, only to blow apart everything I've worked to build in one, stupid night? No, I wouldn't. Viktor is to blame for this. Georg was only defending Pam, and Evan was only trying to break the fight apart."

"Well, I'm not convinced you're not a social media liability to me, now," she said with a constipated, pursed-lip look stuck on her face.

"I'm sorry, Fiona, but that's bullshit." I felt my face go hot. "I've been online all night, and I can attest that ninety-nine percent of people commenting and sharing are saying how horrible Viktor's actions were, and how chivalrous it was for Georg and Evan to step in and defend our honor. While it's unfortunate that it happened at all, it's certainly bound to blow over quickly, and with limited negative effect on the Crush."

"You are our social media manager and you were out with two of our star players—drunk and getting into a bar fight," Fiona snapped. "Your tits were practically hanging out of your dress, Holly."

"First of all, none of us were drunk. We hadn't even been there that long. Viktor came over and insulted my friend and me. The guys tried to shut him up. Yes, things escalated quickly. Yes, we should have just left. But it doesn't change the fact that Viktor caused all of this. And the length of my dress is completely irrelevant. I was out on a date with my boyfriend and off the clock."

"You don't get it, do you? You are never off the clock when you're with the players that you're supposed to be promoting as part of your job. I don't care that you're fucking one of them. I don't care if Max Terry thinks your Evan's his number one lucky charm. I just care that you were out with them on All-Star weekend, and that right now you're all at the center of every top sports story out there. I hired you to help make our team look good."

"I do. I work my ass off, Fiona, and you know it. You know I'm killing every other team when it comes to engagement. You know my strategies have helped increase ticket sales. I produce revenue for this organization. I am really good at what I do, and I won't let you belittle my work just because you're pissed that Max let me date Evan."

The conversation continued only a few moments longer, because Fiona got a call and dismissed me with the wave of a hand. I wandered off, fielded a few questions, bought an Anaheim hat, and disappeared into the stands to cover the skills competition for our social media accounts.

All day, though, I've been bothered by only one part of her ridiculous tirade. The part where she said I'm never off the clock when I'm with the players I'm supposed to be promoting. There is a small sliver of that statement that rings true to me. Can I ever just be Holly, out on a date with my boyfriend, Evan? The reality is we are a well-known couple now. Not celebrities, but close, and people will be watching us. And if I'm working for the Crush, and my love life is intertwined with it, how can we ever disentangle the two things from each other?

I don't think I could just go find another job right now. Not after this snafu with the bar fight. It will blow over; I'm totally positive of that. But for now, I need to hang tight and do the best job I can, like I always have. And since I need to stay put, it really just leaves one option.

I'm going to have to break things off with Evan.

I wait until after dinner to text him.

Holly: Sorry, busy day. Good job out there.

Evan: Thanks

Holly: Are you in your room?

Evan: Yes

Holly: Mind if I pop over to talk?

Evan: That's fine

Great. He's pissed. Maybe it will make this easier.

You know it won't.

I knock on the door to his suite and he opens. He's shirtless and achingly attractive. He basically opens the door and then turns his back on me, wandering barefoot over to the couch, where he flops down and puts his feet on the coffee table.

"You had a good day on the ice," I say, hovering awkwardly by the door.

"Where were you?" he asks stiffly without looking at me.

"In the stands, like I always am."

"I didn't see you. I looked and you were nowhere. And I texted. And I called. No response."

"I'm sorry, Evan."

"I was worried about you!" he shouts angrily. "And I was under a ton of bloody pressure today and I could have used your support. Instead, my head was about half in it and I spent the other half worrying you'd been sacked."

"I wasn't fired, though Fiona threatened it. And of course, you're right. I should have checked in with you. I just felt like laying low. I'm very sorry for ignoring you."

"Well, I'm glad you weren't sacked." He finally looks at me, but his voice still has an edge. I've hurt him, and I feel like even a bigger bitch for what has to come out of my mouth next.

"The thing is, Evan, I don't...I don't see how we can continue this relationship. We're too high profile and our relationship is too wrapped up in the social media of the team. I need to be able to do my job and not have it interfere with my love life."

172

"So, you're saying what?" he asks, his jaw set in a hard edge.

"I'm saying I think we should hit the brakes. We haven't been dating very long. We can just...take a break. Give it some space. Maybe reassess if I can find a different job after the season."

He looks totally shocked. And hurt. I watch the emotions play over his features for several heartbeats before he finally says, "That's total crap."

I laugh a little at the response. "It's...crap?"

"Rubbish," he says. "You think we can just make it stop? Stop caring for one another? Just like that? And you'll go back to just being an invisible cubicle girl who posts some pictures on social media? And I'll pretend I haven't just had my heart ripped to shreds by the first woman I've lov—cared about, in a very long time?"

He was going to say loved. *Loved.* And he stopped himself. It takes my breath away.

"No," I say, my voice small. "I'm not...I'm not trying to hurt you, Evan."

"Look, I realize I pursued you," he says. "I know you dated me against your better judgment. And I know you love your job and you're the best thing since tea and biscuits at it."

"The saying is, the best thing since sliced bread."

"Holly baby," he says, shaking his head at me. "This is not funny. You could literally go work for any team, anywhere. Get a new fucking job."

"You get a new fucking job," I say, giving him a face. "Are you kidding me?"

Evan rolls his eyes. I feel guilty for enjoying his cuteness even when he's this upset. I'm going to hell for sure.

"This is stupid, Holly. Last night was stupid. It's going to be totally off the radar in a day. Don't overreact."

This is basically what I said to Fiona. And I believe it, too. But I'm so confused right now. I care for him so much. And I know he cares about me.

"I just...let me think about this. Let me get some air. We can talk again when we're back home. Okay?"

"Whatever," he says, focusing his angry gaze on some speck of nothing on a far wall.

"I care about you, Evan. Very much. If nothing else, I hope you know that."

He doesn't react to my words. Just a great painful silence across a huge gaping hole of insecurity that has opened up between us.

I leave without hearing his response. If there even was one.

A CAB TAKES me to Pam's apartment, but she's not there. I know where her spare key is hidden, so I grab it and let myself in. I order a pizza, drink a beer, and watch reality television, a guilty pleasure allowed only because I'm feeling totally heartbroken right now.

The entire evening, I alternate between being totally resolved about breaking up with Evan, and being certain I'm making the mistake of a lifetime by dumping my soul mate. Then spending a half-hour ugly crying about it. After about six rounds of this insanity, I finally fall over sideways on the sofa and crash into an exhausted sleep.

When I wake up, my alarm is going off telling me it's time to get ready for another busy day at the arena covering the three exhibition games. Pam never came home, and while I might normally think she's at the hospital or studying, the presence of her laptop and medical bag tells me she's out doing very non-educational things. Possibly with Georg.

That's certainly a conversation waiting to happen, but definitely another time.

The games are exciting and fast-paced. The Pacific division easily beats the Metropolitan team. Atlantic loses, then, to Central division. This is quite an upset, actually, and it creates a real social media fury that I take advantage of while I hype up the Pacific crowd, particularly those who follow the Crush and our players.

When the buzzer blows to start the final game, Evan and Georg play to the crowd with fancy footwork and great passing. They score twice, easily, and the line changes to let the second string of All-Stars in. The game is super exciting and fast, and I get some really great shots for the Instagram account. At one point, Evan looks right at me as I snap a shot. He looks intense, and the photo is perfect, but I know that look is for me, and it makes my stomach twist into a tight knot.

Pacific wins, which is thrilling from a team perspective. I'm so proud of Georg and Evan for leading the team to a win, but so sad because I want to be down on the ice, kissing him, congratulating him, celebrating with him.

I watch from the stands as they do a little closing ceremony, and once the whole thing is over, I pack up and head out, choking back the hot tears that want to make an appearance.

I'M BACK AT work bright and early the next day, bombarded immediately with questions from the office staff about the bar fight. After telling the story for about the twelfth time, I fill up my coffee cup and slide into my chair, happy to be back in my little cubicle and focused on our media plan for the last few months of a very long season.

Work keeps me centered, makes me happy. For the most part, since every bit of the plan has some element of Evan Kazmeirowicz in it. I work dutifully until lunch, then take my usual walking break so I can call Pam.

We make small talk for a few minutes, and then I ask, "Where were you the other night? I let myself in and fell asleep on your couch, but you never came home."

"I was out," Pam says.

"Obviously," I say. "And not at school or hospital. Were you with Georg?"

"I was," she says.

"And you're not going to tell me about it?"

"Nope."

"That's...not like you, Pamela, normally you're all about the kissing and the telling," I tease.

"Who says we were kissing?"

"Wow. Okay. Well, you should know I broke things off with Evan."

"Why?" she asks, genuinely surprised.

"Because my love life cannot be intertwined with my job, and since my job and Evan are basically in the same place, I have to make a choice."

"Sorry, but that's dumb, Holls. Definitely not a good reason to leave someone you love."

"I d-d-don't love him." But I'm lying, so my voice breaks. I clear my throat, hoping I sound convincing, but she's my best friend and she knows me better than that.

"Liar."

"I'm not...we never declared our love for each other. We dated for a few months. And that relationship was affecting my work, so I'm choosing my job over a relationship that was probably about to run its course anyway." My words sound horrible and mean even to my ears.

"Why? Because he's a player and players don't change? Because you're just waiting for him to dump you, so you decided to get the jump on him and dumped him first?" Pam lets me have it. "Have you seen how that man looks at you? He's not going anywhere."

A lump forms in my throat and it takes everything I have to swallow it down and not break down out here in the Las Vegas sun, with the guy from the hot dog truck staring at me. I toss him three bucks and he makes me my usual.

I can't eat it, though. After Pam and I finish our conversation I feel truly sick. Sad and anxious and sick, and knowing without a doubt that I very much want Evan in my life. Is it too late?

Because I'm not second-guessing myself to the nth degree, I'm way less productive and way more mopey in the office the second half of the day. And it's made worse when I head to the restroom only to come out and find Kacey King standing in the lobby, talking to Fiona.

She stomps right up to me and sneers. "Well, I hope you're proud of yourself." I bet she was one of those girls in high school who challenged other girls to fight her behind the gym after school.

I feel my upper lip curl in response. "Excuse me?" She's got no authority over me.

"All-Stars is a really big honor, Holly. And I happen to know that this is something Evan's been working to for much of his career. He's dreamed of this, and you ruined the whole experience for him. You're supposed to protect these players and make them look good. Instead, you almost got him barred from playing. And he looked terrible out there, like he could barely see out of that eye. I can't believe you let him get into a fight like that. And in a public place. You should know that people will be recording with their phones."

"Wow, that was a nice monologue," I answer with as professional of a tone as I can muster. "Except, aren't you a journalist? Shouldn't you be fair and unbiased and using fact in your reports? Because, first, I can't imagine that he was dreaming of the NHL All-Stars while he was on an Olympic team. And, second, he wasn't even close to being barred from play this past weekend. And, third, I didn't let him do anything, nor did I ruin his experience. He played well and his team won."

"Say whatever you need to in order to feel okay about what was an epic fail on your part as social media manager," Kacey says snottily. "You should be fired, in my humble opinion."

"You mean your overblown, worthless, and jealous opinion?"

Kacey gets right in my face. So close that I can smell her cinnamon gum. "You're a novelty. A good girl. Men like Evan dabble in good every so often, but they always go back to bad. He's a good lay, right? I get why you're trying to hold onto him, but let's be honest. You're milquetoast. Boring. Vanilla. And I've still got tricks up my sleeve. He'll be back in my bed in no time."

"Well, I wish you luck with that," I say, starting to turn away.

Kacey grabs me, her nails digging into my upper arm. I spin back as she says, "When I get done with you, you'll have no job and no boyfriend. You'll be able to go back under whatever rock you crawled out from under and that's about it."

I don't know what comes over me. Maybe it's her words, but probably it's the smug look on her face and the fact that she's already opened the door by putting her hands on me, but I slap her across the face.

She lets go and stumbles back, her mouth in an O of shock. Fiona steps in front of me, and says, "Kacey, I think it's time for you to leave. I don't know why you think it's okay to harass one of my employees, but it's not. And furthermore, your access to players will be very limited from now on."

Fiona turns her back on Kacey and gives a little wave for me to start moving. We walk all the way through the office area and into her office, where she shuts the door before heading to her office chair.

"Have a seat," she says, pinching the bridge of her nose between her fingertips.

I sit, still a little dumbfounded by everything that just happened.

"So, I think we should just talk for a minute," Fiona finally says, her tone surprisingly gentle.

"I'm so sorry I slapped her. That is so not like me." I feel truly sick to my stomach.

"Well, normally I would not ever support one of my staff getting physical with a member of the press, since our jobs are to develop relationships with those folks...but I'd say a good slap across the face was warranted in this case. She kinda had it coming."

I feel my shoulders drop as I start to relax. I cannot believe Fiona is defending me. "You have no idea. But I'm still really embarrassed. I'm so sorry, Fiona."

"Just...stop. You have no reason to be sorry. Kacey was out of line and professionally inappropriate. And she put her hands on you first, so it was really self-defense."

"Thank you." We both sit, thinking, for a moment before I say, "I really do love this job, Fiona. I know things have been totally weird, but I hope you can see I care about doing the best for the Crush."

"You are very good, Holly. I'll be honest and tell you it was never your work I had a problem with—it was your relationship with Evan."

I nod, unsure what to say. I end up saying, "Well, the team policy..."

She interrupts. "Forget the team policy. You don't think staff and players hook up all the time? It happens. The policy is supposed to deter it, but sometimes people find each other attractive. I mean, even I have experience with it."

My eyes go wide. "Really? Aren't you married?"

She gives me a frown. "I am. Before I met my husband, I was new here and I was dazzled by the players. And one of them made a beeline for me at every press event. He would flirt and I'd feel great about it, and we started sneaking around, having an affair. It lasted a couple of months before his wife found out about it."

"Oh...Did you know about the wife?"

She shakes her head. "No clue. And most people probably knew about it, but no one said a thing. So I ended up looking like some kind of homewrecker. And I was heartbroken, too. I really cared about him, or I thought I did at the time, anyway."

"I'm sorry that happened to you." And I really am sorry for her, but then a horrifying thought pushes into my head and I have to ask, "Evan's not married, is he?"

She laughs lightly. "No, he's not."

"Good," I say, unable to hide my relief.

"I have to admit my own situation had me already on edge about player/staff relationships, but if I'm being truly honest I also need to admit...my husband and I have not been in a good place recently, and I was jealous. I was jealous of the effort he was putting in to get your attention. I wanted that in my own life. Strange how much I let it affect my behavior and judgment. I apologize for that."

She catches my gaze and holds it for a moment. We both take a few minutes to contemplate before she says, "You really are one of the best young media managers in the game right now, Holly. I'm sorry I haven't been as supportive of your good work as I should have been. I had great female role models and mentors throughout my career and I've really not offered the same support to you. I'm ashamed of it, and I promise I'll do better from here on out."

"Thank you so much, Fiona, it means a great deal to me to hear that from you." I try to overcome the growing pit in the bottom of my stomach. "And by the way...I broke things off with Evan. Before we left Los Angeles. You were right—it's too hard to have a relationship with a player and be in this job. I won't let it happen again."

"Oh, Holly," she says emphatically. "No. No."

"No?"

"I was upset at the situation and I overreacted. Even I can see that Evan is a different man with you in his life. He loves you. And I know you must love him. This is a blip and it will pass, but finding real love like that? You can't give it up just for a job. And your job is not in jeopardy here, so I think you need to go find him and make it work."

"It might be too late," I say sadly, afraid to believe I might be right.

"I doubt that very much." Her phone pings with a text and she says, "I've got to get back to work, and so do you. I'll touch base with you before you leave for the day."

I nod and get up, heading back to my desk. There's a text from Troy, checking in to make sure I'm okay after the bar fight. I respond, telling him the story and letting him know I'm okay. He says he'll be in town for the next home game and wants to sit with me in the stands and then grab a late dinner afterward. This sounds great because I really miss him and can use his advice right about now.

After the day is done and I'm in my car, as soon as I turn on the engine, Justin Bieber's, *Sorry* plays on the radio.

Perfect.

Don't mistake me. I'm not really a Belieber, or whatever his fans are called, but the lyrics are completely relevant to my life right now. *I know, I know that I let you down. Is it too late to say sorry now?* And I want nothing more than to call Evan right this instant to tell him I'm sorry I acted like a scared fool.

But if he will ever be able to forgive me is something completely different.

TWENTY-FOUR

HOLLY

I haven't slept more than a couple of hours the past three nights. I toss and turn, check my phone, and scroll through the social feeds a hundred times instead. I've typed at least ten texts to Evan, and then deleted every one of them. Each long and tortuous night.

It's clear both my heart and my head are leading me back to him, but with each day that passes, I worry more and more that I've probably ruined the best relationship I've ever had.

It's game day, so I need to focus on getting our pre-game feeds up before I meet Troy in the stands. We've got dinner plans right after the game, and I'm really looking forward to getting his advice on this whole situation.

Evan hasn't texted me since Los Angeles. He's been quiet on social media, and while I've seen plenty of photos of some of our other players out in the party scene, he hasn't popped up in any of them. I don't know what to make of this, and when I call Pam about it, she's not really that helpful.

"You did it, Holls." She doesn't spare me even a tiny bit. "Now you've got to eat crow and make it better."

"How do I start? What do I say?" And I really do not know how *make it better*, in her words.

182

"Maybe something like, 'I jumped the gun and acted a fool. I should not have broken up with you?'"

"That's..." I sigh. "Has Georg said anything about it?"

"How do you know I've even talked to Georg?" Her voice is heavy with annoyance, and I suddenly realize that the annoyance might not be directed toward me.

"Is everything okay?" I ask. "I mean...it seemed like you two were enjoying each other's company."

"He's a complicated guy, and I barely know him."

"Really?" I ask, sounding incredulous even to myself.

"There's really nothing to talk about Holls, truly."

"Okay, but if you ever change your mind, I'm here."

After we hang up I'm still left in limbo about how reach out to Evan and close the distance between us.

It's a beautiful day, so I decide to take a run to try to mellow some of the anxiety I'm feeling. I run about seven miles before returning to the arena and heading into the ladies' locker room for a shower. I dress in a short, black skirt, black Vans, and an off-shoulder Crush t-shirt that's tied at one side. I pull my hair into a ponytail, put on a tiny bit of makeup, and head out into the tunnel to get some early Snapchat shout-outs.

The guys are all lined up and I can see Evan at the back of the line with Chalamet. As the team's opening song comes on, the guys start heading out, giving me thumbs-up and waves as they pass. My heart stops in my chest when Evan passes. He stops for a moment and there is nothing but longing and want and hurt on his face. He doesn't seem angry. He just stares into my eyes for a long time, the electricity thick between us.

"I'm sorry for everything I s-s-said to you," I manage to whisper before swallowing the enormous lump in my throat, my heart surely cracking in two. "Go get 'em out there."

He nods once before skating out to the roar of our hometown fans as the pre-game ceremony starts.

I run up to my seat and find Troy already there. He pulls me into a hug and asks, "Evan joining us tonight?"

I shake my head, the lump in my throat growing larger by the second. "We're—we're not..."

"Okay." He pats my knee, which is shaking like crazy. "It's okay. We'll talk about it."

I nod again and the game starts. I'm so thankful, honestly, because it gives me something to focus on. But my heart continues to beat wildly throughout the whole game, especially if Evan looks up at me whenever he gets a chance.

"I'm not in any way an expert on relationships or love, Holly dolly, but I'd say he misses you," Troy comments after the team breaks before the third period.

"You want to head off to dinner early?" I ask him. "I don't have any post-game duties and I've got everything I need for social. I can post the scores and final few promos during dinner, once the game is over."

"That's fine," he says, standing and leading me out.

We end up deciding to walk the mile or so to the restaurant. As we walk, I tell him all about how things went down after the incident at the bar. I fill him in on my decision to break things off, and about what Fiona said to me after the flare up with Kacey.

After I finish my story, he asks, "But are you in love with him?"

"I am." I realize it feels wonderful to admit that out loud to another person. "I haven't wanted to name it. It seemed far too soon or too risky. But I am in love with him. And I miss him very much, but I still don't know how to make it right."

"I think you just need to tell him. Tell him how you really feel."

It's such simple advice, but he's right.

We eat at a small Italian restaurant that's got a couple of screens along the bar. One has the game on, and I watch Evan pummel a guy into the glass—and get a penalty called on him. He sits in the box, seething, while Vancouver goes on a Power Play. When he comes back out on the ice, he's all business, skating fast and tight, taking shot after shot on goal, scoring three times in five minutes.

The game ends with the Crush winning by one point.

I post our end-of-game updates on all of our feeds, and then put my phone down and ask Troy about his most recent recruiting efforts. He's puts up a hand, though, as he peers at the television, even getting up and asking the bartender to turn it up. I follow him to the bar where we watch Chalamet take press from the ice. It's a weird thing, because normally they let the guys shower first then head in for press wrap-up.

Chalamet talks about how exciting this season has been and how happy he is that he gets to go out on a year when the team is playing like one unit. The reporter, a guy from ESPN, turns the camera on Evan. His hair is matted with sweat and the bruise around his eye is a weird purply-green color. But he's smiling, and his eyes are bright. None of that sadness from earlier is there.

I can see other reporters trying to clamber for position with their mics and cameras, including Kacey King, who yells out, "Where did that fire come from in the third period, Evan?"

He doesn't look at her, he continues looking straight at the ESPN camera, and says, "I've had a lucky charm all season. She's totally changed me as a man, and I think as a player, as well. Everything I've done this season, I've done with her at my side. And it was her I was thinking about when I went out there and pushed another win through for our team."

I put my hand over my mouth as a surprised, emotional gasp escapes. I want to cry. I probably will cry. Troy puts his arm around me.

"I love you, Holly Laurent!" Evan yells into the camera. Then he gives a lopsided grin that makes my stomach flutter and says, "Tweet that!"

I laugh and cry at the same time, and without thinking too hard about it I thank Troy for dinner and start running. I run as fast as I can toward the arena to find Evan.

To tell him I love him back.

TWENTY-FIVE

EVAN

I'm looking around, but I don't see her anywhere. I watched her slip out in the third with her uncle, and I'm just hopeful she's catching this live from wherever they landed.

I need to see her. I need to confirm that what I saw on her face in the tunnel was real. I saw it when she said she was sorry. And I didn't even need her to say she was sorry. I just needed to see something that showed me she still wanted me.

Kacey looks utterly disgusted right now, which makes me weirdly happy as I trail the others back down the mirrored tunnel to the locker rooms. I get ribbing after ribbing about my declaration of love, but it doesn't bother me even a little bit. I know most of the guys are truly happy for me.

I take my time in the shower, and by the time I finish getting dressed, I'm one of the last ones out. It's okay, though, because the moment I step out of the locker room and into the hallway, I see her. She's so cute with her Crush t-shirt and her ponytail, and it's only heightened by the anxious look on her face, a look that fades as soon as she sees me.

She runs. Full-on runs. She jumps into my arms, her legs around my waist, her mouth on mine. I hold her so tightly as we kiss that I'm worried I might break her, but I can't loosen up, can't let go. The minute I let those words out into the world, my only hope was she would hear them and come back. And she has.

She eventually slides her feet back to the floor. I rest my chin on top of her head.

"You heard my message?" It's a stupid question. Of course she heard it.

"I heard it and I loved every word of it," she says, kind of muffled because her face is buried in my chest. She backs away—only slightly because I refuse to let go just yet. "I'm such an idiot, Evan. I'm so sorry. I was scared."

"I know," I say, planting a kiss on the top of her head. "I know. I get it. The whole situation was fucked up."

"We're trending," she says with a beautiful Holly-smile. "You made several housewives in Iowa spontaneously combust with that big display, I'm hearing."

I laugh at this. "I think I made Kacey King explode, too. But not in a good way."

"Good way for me," she says resolutely.

"So, I have a question for you." She looks up at me expectantly. "Would you like to see my apartment, Holly?"

"Finally! I was starting to get paranoid, Evan." She looks so sexy when she laughs, it's all I can do to keep things G-rated until I can get her all to myself.

So, I kiss her softly once on the lips and take her hand in mine as we head out of the arena to my car. The drive is short as it always is, and Holly wastes no time picking up on the fact my commute to work is pretty much nonexistent. "Evan! Why do you drive to work when you could walk this route in less than twenty minutes?" She's a smart one, my Holly.

"Because I like my car?" I whine like a child, pushing my lips into a pout just to make her smile. "And I did walk to work...once."

Holly rolls her eyes at me, a sexy smirk on her beautiful face. We hold hands as we head into the elevator, and once those doors close us in I have her pinned to the wall; my hands on her face and my tongue in her mouth. When the elevator pings and the doors open, we all but run to my door.

Inside, she takes a minute to analyze the space. It's a really open floor plan, with a large living, dining, and kitchen area framed with a wall of floor-to-ceiling windows that look out over the Strip. It's not a huge space, but it's got a great view. I'm kind of a minimalist, so my furniture is really basic, my walls very neutral. I have a few pieces of artwork that remind me of home, lots of books on the shelves, a Peloton bike in one corner next to a rack of hand weights.

I show her around, my bedroom is big but not ridiculously so, again very sparsely decorated, with a California King bed covered in a down comforter. My bedroom has the same view as my living room, with black-out curtains to shut it all out as needed.

"This is a nice place, Evan." She eyes the bed and grins, "And that's a pretty big bed."

"I'm a pretty big dude," I say, pulling her into my arms. "There's something else you should know, too."

"Oh?"

"It's new. The bedding, the mattress...all new since I got back from LA."

TWENTY-SIX

HOLLY

Evan Kazmeirowicz is blushing. He's just told me he replaced his whole bed in the past week, and he's blushing about it.

I reach up and rub my thumb over the pink that has bloomed high on his cheeks. "Are you embarrassed? Why are you blushing? That's my thing."

"I just needed to shed the past," he says earnestly. "I wanted to bring you here and have you know this is our space—only for us."

"I am over all of that, truly. Your past—it was who you were then, but it's not who you are now. I trust you." It feels wonderful to say those words to him and to really believe them with my whole heart.

"I know." He cups my face with both of his hands, his thumbs caressing lovingly over my cheekbones, and insists, "But it was important to *me*. I believe you'll be the last woman I ever invite into this bed. It's important to me that you know you are also the first."

The first and the last.

I open my mouth but literally nothing comes out. What can a person possibly say to such a statement? I settle for, "I love you, Evan. I haven't said it yet, but I do. I love you so much."

Evan's mouth is on mine immediately, his hands gripping my ass as he picks me up and carries me into his very large master *en suite*. Still kissing me, he manages to reach into his shower to turn on the water.

"I've been wanting to do this for so long," he says. "Shower with you. Is that weird?"

"*Weird Science*," I say, then giggle. "Sorry, that was dumb."

"I love that movie, it's hilarious!"

We throw movie quotes back and forth and I fall a little more in love with him with each one. Finally, he tests the water and says it's ready. My shirt is over my head—my skirt lying on the floor in a heartbeat. As I stand in front of him, clad only in the lacy black bra and panties I wore in hopes I might end up with him like this, I feel exposed in ways I never have before. I feel like he can see inside of me, and it's so scary, but also so wonderful and freeing. I feel like there is no barrier between us at all now, as if we're really walking a path toward something good together.

"Have I ever mentioned how beautiful you are?" Evan asks as he traces a long finger over the swell of my breast.

"Maybe once or twice," I say, arching into his caress.

He begins undressing me as I take in the view. And my view is pretty magnificent. This beautiful man standing before me has told me he's in love with me. It might take me a bit before I stop pinching myself to see if I'm dreaming or not.

He kisses my neck as his hands reach around to unhook my bra. The sound it makes as the snaps separate before it falls to the floor, makes me shiver beneath his lips. I feel his big hands drawing down my panties, so I help the process along with a shimmy. Completely naked, we step inside the steamy shower. I put my head under the shower head, letting the water soak my hair wet before I push it all back and away from my face. I find Evan staring at the way my breasts jut toward him when my back arches. He looks a little wild and it only makes me hotter knowing he might lose control a little. I love everything about my dominant lover.

He puts some shampoo into his hand and starts working it through my long hair. He massages my scalp, my temples, my neck. I arch back under the spray again to rinse away the soap and feel his fingers playing at my nipples. It's so good feeling his hands on me. My nipples bud up tight, the tips pebbled almost to the point of pain until he takes one in his mouth and twists the other between his fingers.

I hear my cry at the exquisite mix of ecstasy and pain. I want to come, but I want this pleasure-torture to go on forever. *Choices.*

Evan's massive cock is fully erect and jutting in my direction, so I take some body wash and rub my sudsy hands along the length of that huge, beautiful part of him that owns me. He groans and moves closer, putting his forehead on mine as we touch each other. Our hands go where we want and need them to go.

He spins me around after a long, quiet moment of touching. He rubs bubbles and suds all over my breasts and stomach, working his fingertips over my ultra-sensitive flesh before moving down to my sex. He starts outside, his fingers massaging just the folds and my inner thighs. I sag into him because it feels so good I can barely stand. But my body wants more; the ache of want strong and hot between my legs. I open for him, just enough, and his fingers push inside. My hips move in a seductive dance against his fingers, welcoming him to explore at will.

Just as I feel the quake of orgasm begin, he removes his fingers, and spins me around to face him once more. He picks me up as if I'm a feather, lifts me over his twitching cock, and slides his way up into me deep. I wrap my arms around his neck, my legs around his waist. With him buried as far as he can go, we're as close as humanly possible.

He moves slowly, in no hurry for our connection to end. He kisses at my neck, along my jaw. Our tongues connect. My breasts press against his chest. His hands splay along my backside.

His movements grow faster, harder. I urge him to give me more. I want him wild and uncontained.

I flex my pelvic muscles, pushing my body toward that perfect and divine precipice. When I fall, I fall hard, my breath stopping, the noises escaping my throat nearly inhuman. I focus on what Evan is saying to me and then I hear it.

"Holly—Holly—Holly..." My name becomes his mantra, flowing from his lips repeatedly as I struggle to stay earthbound. "I love you," comes out in harsh breaths as he empties himself into me.

He holds me for a long time afterward, until his ragged breathing finally calms. When he finally sets me down, I feel wobbly as jello and have to brace my hand on the wall to help me return back down to earth.

As the hot water pours down upon us, he says, "I will never get tired of you like this."

"Neither will I." And I know I won't as he tilts my chin up to meet his lips for more kisses. I remind him how much I love him.

Evan kisses me until the water goes cold.

Afterward, we curl up in his brand-new bed with pizza and beer, and even find *Weird Science* on demand.

The perfect night.

TWENTY-SEVEN

EVAN

Three minutes until buzzer. Three minutes until that cup is mine.

New York versus Las Vegas. Viktor Demoskev is back on the ice for this final, championship game. He's played well, though the fire has gone out from the hate between him and Georg since the incident in Los Angeles.

We are tied one-one. This is a big game, and while everyone is fired up, no one has gotten past the defensive lines tonight. The goalies have been on fire, diving for saves, keeping access to the goals limited. They are the game MVP's for sure. But I have another MVP title in mind.

I need to score another goal and win this championship.

A high sticking penalty is called on a New York player and seconds later, a cross-checking penalty that puts us into a sizable Power Play.

This is it.

I look up at the owner's box and see Holly up there, jumping and cheering. I grin and get my head back in the game, taking a pass from Georg and practically flying down the ice. The goalie looks ready for me to slam it at him, but I don't. I do a quick pass to rookie Mikhail over on the other side and before the goalie even realizes I don't have the puck, Mikhail wings it right in behind his back.

The crowd goes nuts. Georg looks shocked that I let that goal go to a rookie, but I feel good about it. He was in the right place at the right time and that is how you play the game.

We set up to finish out the last minute, which goes by without another score, but in the end, I don't care. We won.

Georg and I are selected to "hoist the cup," so we shoulder it and skate around the rink as the crowd cheers. I can see the management and media team freaking out up in the box. Max Terry might even be ugly crying. I can't wait to celebrate with my girl.

WE DO OUR usual shower-first-media-second routine, but this time, the whole team is invited in. We all line up, and of course they put Chalamet and me in front of the mics.

A reporter yells out, "Did you engineer that breakaway and fake?"

I shake my head. "Not really. We've played extremely well as a team all season. We have a good sense of space and of how each other's minds work. Those goalies were on fire this game and I knew I wasn't getting a straight shot, no matter how fast I skated. Not tied up and with only minutes left, he wasn't letting a thing through."

"Mikhail was perfectly placed, though," another reporter comments.

"He was," I say. "I felt him there and knew it was right. We needed a goal and it didn't matter who got it."

"That's what good leaders do. That's why I'm thrilled to leave this team in this guy's hands," Chalamet says. "He's going to be an amazing captain next year!"

The reporters focus on David for a few questions, asking him about his own goal early in the game, and about his retirement plans. Then, out of the blue, a reporter says, "The league has just announced the series MVP. It's Evan Kazmeirowicz."

The room erupts with the snap of cameras and the hype of my team, who all cheer and try to reach over to ruffle my hair or slap me on the back.

We finish press and I take a call from Scott, who informs me that Max has offered a huge bonus based on our conversation earlier in the year.

"So, MVP, what's your off-season look like?"

"Holly and I are heading to Colorado," I tell him. "Going to kayak and hike. Maybe get into some other trouble." Images of making love to Holly out in the wild dance through my head.

"I know I was a bit of skeptic earlier this season," Scott says. "I really am happy for you both. Maybe she is your lucky charm."

She absolutely is.

As I hang up, my phone buzzes.

Holly: Nice game, stud. See you out at the car. Tons of press out here, btw.

There's tons of press inside. I can't imagine who's hanging around outside, but it's good, actually. I have one more thing I need to do in order to make this a perfect end to a perfect season.

The guys and I all wander out to the parking lot, bro-hugging and hand-shaking. Max Terry comes out, and our coaching staff. We all take pictures with the cup before it is whisked off into an armored car to be engraved and then delivered for us to display over the summer.

My white Lambo is parked right where I left it and I'm the first to crane my neck as the door opens. Holly, in a sleek, black dress, steps out of the driver's seat. As she approaches on very high and very sexy heels, the press catch sight of her and start snapping pictures.

She gives me a sexy smile and I decide now is the time. I drop to one knee in front of press and management and teammates. I pull out the ring I bought months ago.

Holly starts crying immediately, her hand over her mouth and her shoulders shaking.

"Holly Laurent, you have changed my life. I'm a better player, a better teammate, and a better person because of you. I'm a much better man, and I want to keep getting better, but only with you at my side. Will you be my wife?"

"Yes," she sobs happily. "Yes! Yes! Yes!"

I stand up and slip the ring on her finger before kissing her thoroughly. I hear a million camera clicks but it doesn't bother me a bit. I have my girl in my arms and she just agreed to marry me. Holly extends her hand and examines the ring intently. I watch her eyes fill with fresh tears and it feels like we are walking on air.

Her friend Pam must have been in the passenger side of the vehicle, because she comes from out of nowhere, demanding to see the ring. She deems it "stunning" and gives us both sloppy kisses of congratulation to our cheeks. Georg is next, and it takes a bit of time for Holly and me to make our way to the car and away from the chaos of the parking lot.

We had planned to go out dancing to celebrate, but I think we both feel like there are other, more important things to do.

OUR CATERING SERVER pops open a bottle of champagne as we make eyes at each other over a candlelit dinner in my suite.

We toast to the beginning of forever.

I stare at my future wife and enjoy the show as she blushes for me. I think about all the ways I want to love her. I wonder what's going through her mind right now.

After our dinner, that was dripping with enough sexual innuendo to make our poor server nearly keel over from embarrassment, I tip her handsomely to go away.

I turn on some music, Keane's, *Somewhere Only We Know* plays softly as I pull my fiancée into my arms. We dance as the lights of the Strip shimmer against the panoramic view through the wall of windows.

"I can't believe how much I love you," Holly says. "I can't believe you're mine."

"I'm yours," I remind her. "For as long as you'll have me."

I slip the dress off her shoulders and bare her golden skin, kissing her shoulder blades as she tips her head back, her long hair like a dark waterfall down her back. That dress, as pretty as it is, looks better on the floor as I gaze at the long lines of her toned body. Her calves are shapely in those high-heeled shoes, and I lobby for those to be the *only* thing she leaves on tonight.

I kiss along each bared inch of her skin. I caress the soft skin of her tight ass. I lick and kiss at her sweet pussy through her soaked, silky knickers.

All in all, I worship this woman. So much so, that I ditch her knickers and pick her up, placing her atop the now cleared dining table. I know where I'll be taking my dessert from tonight—the sweetness between her legs.

"You're a goddess," I say, my beard and lips and tongue coated in her juices. She's boneless from the orgasm I just gave her. I love her this way.

I carry her to my bed and take my time entering her. When I do, I'm looking deeply into her eyes as I fill her up. We are truly one body together. I see a single tear fall from the corner of her eye and onto the pillow.

I make love to this amazing, beautiful woman I never expected to find.

But am so grateful I did.

TWENTY-EIGHT

HOLLY

"So, guess who is the new team physical therapist for the Crush," Pam says on the other end of the line.

"Ummmm," I say, knowing the answer already.

"Me!" she exclaims. "Me! I got the job!"

"I'm so psyched for you. And we get to work together. Kind of."

"I know, I can't believe it. I've wanted to work in a sports shop forever. I can't wait to get started."

"Are things going to be okay...working with Georg?" I ask carefully.

"Meh, I can handle him."

"No doubt you can, friend."

"What's up with you?" she quickly changes topics. "How's it feel to be engaged now that you've had a few weeks to let it all sink in?"

"Great," I answer. "It's been really, really great."

"Okay, Holls, that was a lot of greats, which means something's on your mind. Fess up, girlie."

"No, it's totally perfect. It's just that Evan and I are about to head out to Colorado for a few weeks. He does some off-season training out there and I want to take him hiking and camping and stuff. But I haven't been feeling super great the last couple of days."

"You haven't been feeling well how?" she asks, suspicious.

"Nauseous, tired. Probably the flu."

"Or...not the flu? Maybe you're preggo?"

I open my mouth and then shut it. Then say, "I'm six days late."

"Yup," Pam says. "Go get a test."

"I will. Hey, I've got to run. Got things to buy and clothes to pack."

"Get a test!" she yells. "Go now! Now, I say!"

I laugh and promise I will. She says if I were at her house, she'd let me take one from the stash in her bathroom.

"I'm not sure what level of horrified I am that you have a stash of pregnancy tests in your bathroom at home, Pamela Jenson."

"Don't be judgey, it doesn't suit you at all. That girl from the clinic who roomed with me for a few months left a bunch of tests behind when she bailed. She was weird."

"God, I love you." The fact that she will be in Vegas working for the Crush fills me with happiness.

"Love you too, you little slut who gets knocked up by her fiancé. That's going to be one cute kid."

I try to imagine what my kids with Evan would look like. My tummy does a little flip at the thought. We can't be too shocked, either of us. We've had unprotected sex more than once...that I can remember. Pam's right. I need to take a pregnancy test.

After we say goodbye I drive to the nearest pharmacy and buy two tests. Then I head straight home to my apartment to finish up my packing. I pee on the little plastic stick, lay it on the bathroom counter, and get to work.

An hour later I'm packed and ready, expecting Evan to show any moment, when I wander into the bathroom and see the test lying there on the counter.

I realize I never looked at it.

TWENTY-NINE

EVAN

W e've been driving for about six hours, and now find ourselves on a really windy road toward the Rocky Mountains.

I've rented an amazing villa in the hills which offers us privacy and space to do all of the outdoorsy things that Holly has planned. We've been listening to music all the way, and while she's seemed happy overall, there is definitely something going on with her.

"You okay over there, Champ?" I ask.

"I'm just dandy," she says, just a little too chipper.

"That's a weird word, baby. What's going on? Car sick?"

"You could say that," she says quietly.

"Oh, sorry. We'll be to the house in like six minutes."

She nods, but I can tell there's something she's not saying. I let it go, her spirits appearing to lift as soon as she sees the gorgeous home I've rented for us. Holly's so excited she hops out of the SUV before it's barely come to a complete stop.

I pop open the back end of the new Land Rover, recently purchased for just these sorts of trips, and walk over to Holly where she stands admiring a stunning view of mountains and forest that goes on for days. I wrap my arms around her from behind and rest my chin on the top of her head. "I hope this means you're feeling a little bit better."

"I'll be fine," she says in a quiet voice.

The sound of a bag thumping to the ground catches our attention as her soft luggage tumbles out of the back of the Rover and onto the ground. A few things spill out of the top, which wasn't totally zipped all the way and scatter in the gravel.

She scrambles to grab at something, but I get to it first, struggling to comprehend precisely what I'm looking at. It doesn't take long for me to figure it out, though. I'm not that dumb.

"A pregnancy test." I say, frowning at the white stick.

I look more closely at it. The little window shows a **+** with the explanation key displaying the word "pregnant" beside the **+** symbol.

I look up at Holly.

I look down at that little **+** some more.

Then back up to find her beautiful face again. She's biting her lip and there are tears in her eyes.

"Are you? Are we?" I stammer.

She nods. I can't tell if she's happy or not.

"When...?"

"Could have been any of the times we did it without a condom," she says. "We weren't exactly careful. But I think it was the night after you won the cup."

"So...just a handful of weeks?"

She nods again. "I think. I'll need to confirm with a doctor."

I stare at her for a minute, trying to read her mind. "Are you happy?"

"I'm...shocked. But not unhappy," she says carefully. "I mean, it's not the timing *I* would have picked for us to start a family...this news, our engagement...it's all really...a lot."

"Well, that's certainly a pragmatic approach." I can see she is worried about what I think about it.

"You're not exactly showing your hand, either," she counters. "How do you feel about being pregnant with me? Are you—h-happy?"

I lean in and kiss her sloppily on the mouth. "Are you kidding me? We made a life. We made a baby. And we're getting married. And we love each other. What's not to be happy about any of that?"

I scoop her up, the bags in the back of the car ignored for the moment, as I carry my new little family—now the center of my world—over the threshold.

EPILOGUE

EVAN

I t's almost time to head back to Las Vegas, but first we have
something very important to do.

"Do I look like a dick?" I ask as I straighten my bow-
tie. "Should I have gone for something more casual?"

"It's your wedding day, dude," Georg says. "It's
customary to wear a tux."

"I guess you're right," I say, fiddling uselessly with the tie.

There's a sharp knock on the door that's quickly followed
by Holly's uncle Troy as he steps into the room. "You ready,
Evan?"

"Born ready," I tell him.

He gives me a once-over. "You look good, son. No
nerves?"

He's totally feeling me out. I get it. He's like a father to
her, more than her own father, really. And he'll be the one
giving her away today. He wants to make sure I've really left
behind my womanizing ways. My words, not his. He called me
the night after my very public proposal, asking me if I was
sure, his warning message loud and clear—Do not hurt my
Holly-dolly or I will fuck you up.

"None whatsoever. I've never been more certain of anything in my life."

He slaps me on the back. "Good man. Time to go."

We head out to the sprawling deck off that backside of the villa where we've been staying most of the summer. It's like a second home now and I haven't told Holly, but I've made an offer to buy it as a wedding present to her. It will be our special place to come whenever we need to get away from it all. She'll be able to enjoy the great outdoors to her heart's desire.

Georg and I head down the aisle. There are about fifty guests, some of our closest friends. My parents are here—not speaking but in the same space, so we'll call it a win. Holly's mom is here with her new husband. They've been staying with us for about a week, so we've had a chance to talk a bit. I was surprised to hear the regret in her voice when she spoke to me about her move overseas, about leaving Holly to fend for herself through college. She mentioned missing cross-country meets and wishing she'd been able to be more involved. She's followed Holly's social media feeds since she started at the Crush, even learned to enjoy hockey. I can see she loves her daughter and that makes me happiest of all.

Georg and I line up next to the minister as a string quartet starts playing. The mountain view is amazing. The sky is bright blue. Pam makes her way down to us, looking fantastic in a green dress that flaunts her figure. I side-eye Georg, who's mouth is practically dragging on the ground. I don't know what's going on between those two, but something is for sure.

When Holly steps out of the house in a silky white gown, her hair loose, a flower crown on her head, just the tiniest bump of our baby at her waist, I fall in love with her all over again. There's a huge lump in my throat, which is insane. I never cry. Ever. But I might just now, because this woman is so beautiful, and she is mine. Troy gives her a kiss on the cheek after he brings her to my side, then takes a seat beside to Holly's mom.

The minister talks about respect, partnership, and about being fair to each other. He talks about love, and while I try to pay attention, I just can't stop myself from getting lost in Holly's

CRUSHED

features. Her wide, brown eyes with their tiny flecks of green and gold, her perfect lips. The small freckles that dot her nose and cheeks from days in the sun. The way her breasts curve, now swollen as she carries our child.

When it comes to our vows, we decided to keep it simple, focusing on equality, trust, love, and partnership. I go first, practically ready to yell these vows into the mountains around us. I want everyone to hear me make this commitment. When I slip the ring on her finger, my heart feels like it might beat its way out of my chest.

Holly's gaze has been locked with mine, and it's only when the ring goes on that her signature blush comes out, a small smile playing on her lips. I wink at her and the pink deepens further.

She repeats her vows, and a moment later, I'm wearing my own wedding band. At some point I'm kissing her, and I completely forget where we are. People good-naturedly start clearing their throats to remind me. *Bastards.*

The party goes late into the night, but I made sure to sneak us away at the first opportunity. I need to be alone with my wife. It's been a week since we've had the house totally to ourselves.

As we stand in the bedroom, a high-ceilinged, rustic space that we have enjoyed very much, I take Holly's face in my hands and kiss her. It's light, just a sweet promise of love. I bend down, kissing her belly over the white silk of her wedding dress.

I get undressed quickly, watching as she slips the straps of her dress from her shoulders. It pools like silken water around her feet as it meets my more haphazard pile of pants, shirt and jacket. Her strapless bra barely contains her now-bigger breasts. Her hips are slightly wider below that shapely belly. I lick my lips as I stay on my knees, supplicant to her. I kiss her bare skin. The skin of her calves and ankles. The skin between her legs, her thighs. The skin of her belly. My hands trace the swell of her backside as her hips arch toward me. I remove her lace panties with my teeth, a wicked grin on my face as I bury my tongue exactly where I've needed it to be for the past week.

She moans, her hands on my shoulders as she loses herself against my lips and tongue. I pleasure her thoroughly, not satisfied until I taste her orgasm.

We move to the bed, where Holly climbs atop me, guiding me inside her as she takes control. She rides me, her hands bracing on my chest as if she's taking ownership of me. It's the ultimate turn-on to see her like this, our bodies connected so deeply. Her rhythm is slow and unhurried, and I just enjoy the feeling of her, my hands roaming over her perfect skin wherever I need to touch. She builds herself up again before my thumb finds her clit, putting pressure on that magical little love button I know will push her over the edge.

She cries out my name as we come together. I am speechless as I witness the look of utter possession on her face. I love this woman so much.

Eventually we come down from the pleasure and fall into a wonderful tangle of arms and legs, both of us whispering words of love and commitment in between a thousand kisses.

I am awake for a long time after she falls asleep. Just watching her breathe. I can't believe I found her. I can't believe she's mine.

Crushed from the moment I laid eyes on her for the first time.

Utterly and happily crushed.

THE END

ABOUT THE AUTHOR

Brit DeMille is the alter ego of a *NYT* Bestselling author having a blast writing something different than what she usually writes. Brit loves stories about sexy billionaires [millionaires make the cut too] who fall in instalove with young women who may or may not be virgins, and then go on to make adorable babies together. In addition to billionaires, hot hockey players are at the top of her list of favorite heroes, along with royals and ex-military bodyguards.

The most important thing to Brit when she writes a story is a happily ever after. But during the actual *writing* of the story, the most important thing to Brit is a cup of hot tea with a splash of milk, and a stash of cherry Jolly Ranchers. A dog or two will likely be in between Brit and the chair at any given moment, which is very handy, because they are the ones who approve everything she writes.

www.britdemille.com

BOOKS BY BRIT DEMILLE

Vegas Crush Hockey Series

CRUSHED
SIN SHOT
RED ROCKET

Standalones

THE BEAUTY & THE BILLIONAIRE
ROOM FOR SIN

84204852R10136

Made in the USA
San Bernardino, CA
06 August 2018